Veronica Moon went to Farnham School of Art and then worked for a number of years in advertising. She is married and lives in Twickenham and now runs her own business in antiques. She has previously had some poetry published, but this is her first novel.

Best wishes
Veronica Moon

To my dear husband and my friends, Heather Morgan and Gilly Spargo, with many thanks for their help and encouragement.

Veronica Moon

THE SCENT OF HONEYSUCKLE

AUSTIN MACAULEY
PUBLISHERS LTD.

A CIP catalogue record for this title is available from the British Library.

ISBN 9781786129215 (Paperback)
ISBN 9781786129222 (Hardback)
ISBN 9781786129239 (E-Book)
www.austinmacauley.com

First Published (2017)
Austin Macauley Publishers Ltd.
25 Canada Square
Canary Wharf
London
E14 5LQ

Jed Fuller was idly waiting for May at the lych-gate while she changed the flowers in the church. He did not like to go in, never feeling comfortable, though whether it was the musty smell that put him off, or the numerous holy images, he could not say.

It was a glorious summer afternoon, the sun high in a clear blue sky, and he thought it was far too good a day to spend indoors, so as he whiled away the time he took out his penknife and began to carve a heart with his and May's initials into the trunk of the old yew tree that stood next to the gate. He was seventeen years old, lean and brown as a nut and, as requested, had brought a trug full of flowers up from the gardens of the manor for the church. The arrangement of these was a task that May particularly enjoyed, as it gave her a rare opportunity to be artistic and create something beautiful that would be appreciated by the community.

When she had finished she closed the heavy oak door behind her, and Jed watched her walk down the path swinging the empty basket on her arm, and he thought how pretty she looked in her light, floral summer frock. The sweetheart neckline framed her face becomingly, and her legs were bare and tanned from the sun, her feet slipped into straw sandals, and she looked as if she didn't have care in the world. She usually wore her hair up in a bun, but today she had plaited it and woven it around her head, and Jed had the sudden urge to unpin it and comb out the thick chestnut tresses with his fingers.

He abandoned his carving of the heart as she approached and asked him, "What are you still doing here?"

He grinned and replied, "Waiting for you o'course." He took the basket from her arm, and a gleam of light reflected from the diamond ring on her left hand caught his eye, and she held it out for him to admire.

"It's lovely, isn't it?" she asked.

"I s'pose," he admitted grudgingly, and then said, "come on, I'll walk you home."

He walked slowly beside her up the lane, and they stopped for a moment as he drew her attention to watch a woodpecker tap-tapping on the trunk of an old tree, and it was then that he asked her for a kiss. She shook her head, shy suddenly, but he persisted, taking hold of her hand.

"Please May," he beseeched, "just give me one kiss."

"No Jed," protested May earnestly. "Don't be silly, you know I'm engaged to James now."

"How could I forget, you keep reminding me every five minutes," he said with exasperation, "but we used to be good pals, didn't we?"

"Yes of course, and we still are," replied May firmly, "but that's all we are." Jed looked down at his boots, crestfallen, trying to think of something that would change her mind.

"I knows I'm not much of a catch," he admitted, "I can't even read and write proper, but I loves you with all my heart, and I'd work hard and look after you. Don't marry him May," he begged. "I knows he's educated but he ain't no good for you, and he won't treat you right."

"But I love him Jed, and he loves me," May insisted "and there's an end to it."

Jed sighed and said with resignation, "All right, I knows when I'm beat. Just give me one kiss then to say goodbye, and I promise I'll not bother you again."

May looked dubious, but then she relented and said, "Alright, but only if you promise not to tell a soul."

"I promise," said Jed, taking her in his arms. She closed her eyes as he tenderly kissed her and for a brief moment the Earth seemed to pause on its axis. Then she pulled away and ran up the lane and he thought *If she turns and looks at me, it will be alright*, but she didn't look back, and he kicked at the base of a tree in frustration, unable to hold back the tears as he gazed after her, and both of them would remember that kiss for as long as they lived.

MAY, VIOLET AND DOREEN

Chapter 1

One day in June 1957 would be indelibly imprinted on the memory of Doreen Bland for the rest of her life. She had gone to the surgery that morning complaining of nausea and loss of appetite and, after a cursory examination, the doctor had told her that she was expecting a baby. Although she had suspected that she might be pregnant, it was still a shock to have it confirmed, and then she had walked home slowly, dragging her feet, trying to think of a way to break the news.

How could she have fallen pregnant when they always been so careful? And then it came to her, it had happened on Ray's birthday when the condom machine in the gents at their local pub had jammed. He had taken her into a dark alleyway and persuaded her to let him have his way, saying, "It'll be alright babe, you won't get pregnant if we do it standing up." Well, so much for that theory!

As she let herself into the house, she was surprised to find that her usually conscientious mother, Violet, had not gone to work but was sitting slumped at the kitchen table, a cigarette burning in her fingers. "Are you ill?" she asked, wondering how she could tell her the news of her pregnancy, when her mother said flatly, "Your Aunt May's dead."

"Oh!" Doreen sat down opposite and let the news sink in. She didn't really know how she felt, for she had never met her aunt, as Violet and her sister May hadn't spoken for years. They had written occasionally, a card at Christmas, and the odd school photo of Doreen, but she had never seen any photos of May, and she never knew the reason for the family feud.

"Here." Her mother pushed an envelope across the table to her. "This came from the solicitors."

Doreen tore open the envelope, her hand shaking a little, and read the letter twice, just to make sure she understood everything. She looked up and saw that her mother was watching her intently. "Well?"

"Aunt May left me Honeysuckle Cottage, and all her possessions," she said softly.

"Well don't sound so surprised," Violet retorted. "Who else would she leave it to?"

"But it's your old home," protested Doreen. "She should have left it to you."

Violet snorted, "She wouldn't have left me even a pot to piss in. I didn't exist as far as she was concerned." Doreen now registered that her mother's eyes were a little red-rimmed from weeping, proof that she had been upset over her sister's death, in spite of the hard, uncaring front she put on.

"Why did you and Aunt May never get on?" asked Doreen tentatively, for it was a touchy subject.

"I've told you before," said Violet tetchily, "it's none of your business. Now, what did the doctor have to say?"

Doreen blanched and fidgeted and could not meet her eyes, and Violet, with razor sharp insight said suddenly, "You've a bun in the oven, haven't you?" Doreen nodded miserably, and her mother asked harshly, "I suppose it's his?"

"If you mean Raymond, of course it's his, who else?"

"Well I hope he'll do the decent thing, but you needn't think you can sponge off me."

"You forget, I've got a cottage now, I don't need your charity," retorted Doreen, and immediately regretted her outburst, for her mother's mouth snapped shut like a steel trap, and she knew she would be given the cold shoulder for the rest of the day.

Violet had little time for Raymond and frequently voiced her disapproval to her daughter. "I don't know what on earth you see in him. You know he'll never amount to anything; he's got no ambition."

"Of course he's got ambitions," countered Doreen hotly.

Violet sneered sarcastically "What, as a grease-monkey? I think you can do a lot better for yourself. What about that nice boy at the bank?"

That 'nice boy at the bank' was someone that Doreen had gone out with a couple of times, but she soon realised that he was definitely not her cup of tea. He was rather shy, had horribly sweaty palms and no idea how to kiss a girl, whereas Raymond had made her go weak at the knees the first time he had kissed her.

Doreen went to her bedroom to decide on her outfit for the evening as she wanted to look her best when she broke the news to Raymond. She picked out his favourite dress, a full skirted one printed with blue flowers, under which she would wear her net petticoats, but when she took them out of the wardrobe she found that they had gone a bit limp, and so she dipped them in a solution of sugar water before hanging them on the line to dry. Then she put her hair in rollers, had a leisurely bath and spent the next half an hour carefully putting on her make-up. By this time the petticoats had dried and stiffened nicely, and when she put them on they swished satisfactorily against her nylon stockings, and content that she looked her very best she left the house, slamming the door in Violet's disapproving face.

She had arranged to meet Raymond at the local pub at half past six. They had been going out for almost a year and he was the only boy she had ever been serious about. She supposed they were going steady, but she wasn't at all sure how he would take her news. Raymond was at present employed on a building site, not a job he enjoyed, but he needed to earn his keep and give his widowed mother some money. His real passion however, was his motorbike and he dreamed of owning a motorcycle showroom and repair shop one day.

When Doreen walked in he was half way through his first pint and turning, whistled appreciatively and gave her a smile that made her heart beat a little faster. He had already bought her a gin and tonic, but she pushed aside the gin and said, "Just tonic for me, Ray."

"What am I going to do with this then?" he asked sullenly, miffed that he had wasted his money.

"Come and sit down, I've got something to tell you," she said softly.

He carried their drinks over to a corner table and sat down, looking at her with anticipation. "What have you got to tell me then?" he asked, and she hesitated, wondering how he would react, and he, with unusual insight, said, "You're not ...."

"Expecting? Yes, actually."

He blew his cheeks out. "Blimey! When's it due?"

"In about six months' time."

He sat silent for a moment, letting the news sink in, and she crossed her fingers and prayed that he would be pleased. Then he gave a broad grin and said, "Hey, I'm going to be a father! I s'pose we'd best get wed then!"

It was a few days later when Raymond Smith eased his bike down the narrow track with Doreen clinging on to his waist for dear life as the wheels bumped over the potholes. They rounded the bend, and there was Honeysuckle Cottage at last! She removed her headscarf and shook out her long, auburn hair and gazed up at her inheritance.

"Ooh Ray, look, isn't it dinky?" she cried, before making her way up the narrow path and fitting the key into the stout oak door. The hinges creaked a little as the door swung open, and she stepped hesitantly straight into the kitchen, which was dominated by a large, cast-iron range and she noticed a faint odour of bacon fat. It was fairly dark and gloomy, for the two small gothic windows either side of the door were dirty and partially overgrown with honeysuckle, and didn't let in a lot of light.

Doreen looked around for the light switch, but there didn't appear to be any electricity, and then she noticed an oil lamp and matches on the pine dresser. As she struck a match, she saw blue and white willow pattern plates ranged along the shelves, and noticed that they were covered in a fine layer of dust. She would have to give everything a good scrub before they could think of moving in, and then Raymond shouldered open the door and rubbed his hands.

"It's a bit parky in here."

"Well, I suppose when the range is lit it would be quite cosy."

"That thing's out of the ark," said Raymond dismissively. "What's in there?" he asked, pushing open the door, and suddenly the room was flooded with light from a huge gothic window with double doors that opened on to a lovely secluded garden.

"Oh golly!" exclaimed Doreen in awe, for the room was light and airy, and in complete contrast to the gloom of the kitchen. Either side of the fireplace were white painted, arched gothic bookcases and she was touched to see some of her school photos ranged along the shelves. The room was rather sparsely furnished however, with just a shabby chintz sofa, a worn velvet rocking-chair, and two small tables. On one of them stood a pretty glass oil lamp of a deep cranberry colour, and on the other a wind-up gramophone.

Doreen was keen to spend some time going through all her aunt's things in order to get to know her benefactress at last, but Raymond was restless and asked, "Where's the khazi then?"

"I don't know, maybe it's upstairs," said Doreen, and added "do you have to be so vulgar? I don't want our baby learning words like that."

They went back into the kitchen and climbed the dark, narrow stairs to the first floor. There they found two rooms of equal size, one of which was her aunt's bedroom and contained a wrought iron double bed, a pine wardrobe and a matching chest of drawers. Ray bounced up and down on the bed and then grinned and pulled Doreen on top of him, saying, "How about christening this then?"

Doreen shook her head and said, "No, stop it Ray, I want to explore." This room had a large window in the

17

gothic style that overlooked the garden, and a small wrought iron balcony that was overgrown with honeysuckle. The other room was very sparsely furnished and had two small gabled windows, and it contained two single beds with a chest of drawers between them, but there was no bathroom.

They went downstairs and out into the garden, and on the side of the house they found an outside lavatory, a wash-house with a tin bath that was full of spiders, and an old-fashioned hand operated mangle, and a wood shed that contained a stock of chopped wood ready for the range.

"How did Aunt May manage without a bathroom?" asked Doreen.

"I suppose she must have had to heat up enough water on the range to fill that tin bath," Raymond shrugged.

"How awful, I don't think I could cope with that," shuddered Doreen.

"Well, if we're going to live here, you'll have to," said Raymond pragmatically, "as we can't afford to put in a bathroom on what I earn."

Doreen was beginning to realise that they would have to put up with the nineteenth century conditions, at least for a while, for once they were married and the baby was born they would not be able to live with her mother, and with Raymond's brother still living at home, his mother's two-bedroom house would not be big enough to accommodate them all. She tried to look on the bright side; at least the village was pretty, with a good pub that served a tasty lunch, and a post office cum general store that would be able to supply most of their needs.

Before they returned home Doreen went upstairs once more to have another look around her aunt's bedroom, and noticing a photograph of a family group on the chest of drawers, took a closer look at it. She recognised her mother, so the other girl had to be May, and the older couple must be her grandparents. She studied May carefully and, realising that she greatly resembled her aunt, was suddenly overcome with a feeling of sadness that she had never got to know her. Well it was too late now.

She opened the wardrobe, running her hand over her aunt's dresses, and then at the back, found a shoebox that contained old letters and photographs, and she recognised her mother's hand-writing on one of the envelopes. Before she could read any of the letters however, Raymond's voice called impatiently up the stairs, "Doreen, can we go now? I'm perished." Sighing with frustration, she tipped the contents of the shoebox into her handbag to read in peace later, and hopefully shed some light on the mystery of the feud between her mother and her aunt.

Chapter 2

Doreen's mother, Violet, worked in Marvel's Modes, which was a rather genteel ladies dress shop in the high street. It was really quite a pleasant job, and she worked Monday to Saturday with Wednesday afternoon off, and a generous 33 per cent discount on clothes. She was a great advertisement for the shop, for almost anything she wore looked good on her tall, elegant frame. She took care to be always immaculately made-up, bleaching her hair as soon as the darker roots started to show and, if she could afford it, treating herself to a manicure once a month.

Mr Marvel was a good employer, and Violet had tried to persuade Doreen to come and work there too. However, being bossed around by her mother day in and day out was the last thing that Doreen had in mind, although she really liked Mr Marvel, or Uncle Harry as she had come to call him. He was a Greek Cypriot who, though he had lived in England for twenty years, had still retained his strong Greek accent, and he had sad brown eyes and thinning dark hair that Doreen suspected he tore out in frustration with his feckless son.

When he first came to this country he had changed his name to Harry Marvel because nobody could pronounce his Greek name, Haralambos Mickaeloudis, and for years now he had looked after his bedridden wife. She suffered from a debilitating muscle wasting disease, and Harry did not have the heart to leave her, although it was now a marriage in name only, and he loved Violet who had been his mistress for the last ten years.

From the first moment she had walked into his shop to apply for the post of sales assistant, Harry had been smitten by her. She had looked coolly elegant, as if she had just stepped out of the pages of Vogue, and she had been honest with him from the start, telling him she was a widow with a young child to support, and would only be available to work during term-time. He had agreed to give her a month's trial, mainly for the pleasure of seeing her again, but she had proved herself to be a hard worker, and he liked her feisty attitude and the way that she dealt with difficult customers.

One young woman in particular regularly gave him a headache. She would buy a dress on a Friday or Saturday, and then return it on Monday, declaring it not suitable and wanting her money back. Harry suspected she wore the article, and would have reimbursed her anyway. Violet, however, had turned the dress inside out, sniffed the armpits and then handed it back to her saying coolly, "This has been worn. I'm sorry Madam, but we only refund on pristine garments." The woman had tried to protest, but Violet had stood her ground, giving only a knowing smile, and the customer, realising she'd been caught at her little game, snatched the dress back and stormed out of the shop. Harry was impressed, and asked her how she'd known the woman had worn it. Violet laughed and said, "Well, I've done the same myself in the past, and there's always a trace of powder or a whiff of sweat under the arms, you can't disguise that."

When she had been working for him for a few weeks, Harry asked her out to dinner, and he found a sympathetic ear to confide his troubles to. He told her about his wife's illness and Violet asked curiously "What's the matter with her?"

"She has a progressive muscle wasting disease," Harry replied. "It began a couple of years after Nicolas was born, and I'm afraid that she will never get better. She already has difficulty eating, and now she can't get out of bed anymore and needs constant care."

He looked so sad that Violet's heart went out to him and she took his hand. "I'm so sorry Harry. It must be very hard for you. How old is your son?"

"He's fifteen, nearly sixteen."

"Is he your only child?"

Harry nodded and confided in her that he was worried sick about him. He sighed deeply and said, "The boy has got in with one of those teenage gangs, and he's already been in trouble with the police a couple of times. I'm just worried that he's going to end up in Borstal. Violet had replied that perhaps it would shock him into turning away from his criminal activities, and Harry said sadly, "I hope you're right, but nothing I say to him makes any difference. I'm only the idiot who pays his fines."

Violet had invited Harry for Sunday lunch the following week, and he met little Doreen for the first time. He was enchanted by her big blue eyes and auburn curls, and on future visits would always bring her a little gift, a book or some coloured pencils, and she looked forward to seeing him for, since Great Grandpa Bland had died, he was the only man in her life that she could relate to.

That first Sunday, after lunch, Violet had sent Doreen round to play with a friend, and somehow she and Harry had ended up in bed together. It was purely sex on her part, but as they had both enjoyed the experience, it then became a regular occurrence, and in time Violet came to grow very fond of Harry, and he plainly adored her.

Doreen somehow knew that Violet and Harry were having an affair, even though nothing had ever been said and once, with childish candour, she had asked her mother "If Uncle Harry's wife dies, would you get married to him?"

Violet had rolled her eyes and said with exasperation, "Oh Doreen, how should I know?" but her daughter would have secretly been pleased, for she thought Harry would have been a kind and indulgent stepfather.

She barely remembered her real father, for James Bland had been killed in the war, and she just had a vague memory of a tall man in scratchy khaki who had carried her round on his shoulders. James had only managed to come home on leave a couple of times, and he could never stay for long, so she never really got to know him. Her mother had told her she had got her cornflower blue eyes and auburn hair from him, but she did not know until she had seen the photo of May where her curvy and full-breasted figure came from.

When Harry heard that Doreen was getting married, he generously allowed her to take the pick of his collection of wedding dresses, as she had set her heart on a white wedding and he knew Violet didn't have much money. It was a bit of a rush to arrange everything before she started showing, as Violet would have been mortified to see her daughter walking up the aisle with a big bump in front of her. Doreen asked Harry if he would give her away, and he was delighted and touched to be asked, his dark eyes welling up with emotion.

The wedding was a small affair, only twenty guests, with the reception held at their local pub. Violet had arranged and paid for the buffet, but Harry very generously offered to pay the bar bill. They were rather short of relatives, with Doreen having just her mother and Violet's best friend Rita who was a surrogate aunt to her, and Harry, who would be in place of her father. On Raymond's side of the family there was only his widowed mother, his uncle, aunt and cousin, and his brother Robert, who was to be best man. The rest of the party was made up of their friends, and Doreen had asked her two best friends to be bridesmaids and, as money was tight, Harry had offered to drive them all to the church in his Rover.

Now, as she stood putting the finishing touches to her hair and pinning on her veil, she felt butterflies in her stomach and wondered, not for the first time, if she was doing the right thing in marrying Raymond, but it was too late to change her mind, as there was the baby to consider. She ran a hand over her stomach, and feeling a little kick she smiled and smoothed down the dress that had been cleverly cut to hide her condition, and nervously touched the gold locket at her neck. It had belonged to her grandmother, and Violet had worn it at her own wedding, but now she had given it to Doreen as something old, a garter being something blue, and she had borrowed the pearl drop earrings that were her mother's favourites.

Violet had been in a funny mood all morning, fussing round and being snippy with everyone, and it was a relief when Harry came to take her and the bridesmaids off to the church. She had looked wonderfully elegant of course, in an ice blue tailored silk suit that brought out the colour of her eyes, and a tiny veiled hat perched at a jaunty angle on her immaculately coiffed blonde hair, but once or twice she had looked perilously close to tears.

Doreen looked critically at herself in the mirror; she would never be elegant, her figure was too full, but she was not displeased with her reflection. She heard a toot on the horn and quickly sprayed on some of Violet's French perfume, and then Harry opened the front door and called to her that it was time to go to the church. As she came downstairs, he drew in his breath and gave a low whistle, saying "My dear, you look so beautiful," and overcome with emotion he dabbed his eyes and said, "I wish that you really were my daughter; I would have been so proud." It was just what she had needed to hear, and she kissed his cheek and told him he would have made her a wonderful father.

As he slowly led her up the aisle and she saw Raymond nervously waiting at the altar, her heart skipped a beat and all her doubts suddenly melted away. He looked so handsome in his new dark blue suit with the velvet collar, the jacket cut fashionably long, and his hair Brylcreemed into a quiff and combed into a DA at the back. She had asked him once quite innocently what DA stood for, and he had laughed and said, "Duck's arse, of course!" And then she had laughed too, for of course, it was obvious. His eyes shone with pride when he saw her, and he whispered "You look a million dollars babe!" and then she knew that everything was going to be alright.

After the reception, when Doreen had changed into her going away outfit, the confetti had been thrown, and Harry had driven the newly-weds to the station, Violet suddenly felt utterly despondent. When he returned she said, "Take me home Harry, I've had it for today." When he had driven her back to the house she unpinned her hat and slumped down on the sofa, and he made them mugs of tea and poured in a liberal amount of whisky, then said, "Come on Vi; shall we drink these upstairs?"

As they got into bed she began to weep, "I've lost my little girl Harry, and I'm all alone; I've got no-one now."

"Don't be silly," he replied, putting an arm round her, "you've always got me, and she'll be back to see you soon enough, especially once the baby is born."

"Yes, of course, you're right." She dried her eyes and gave him a wobbly smile. "I don't know what I'd do without you."

"Likewise," he said, kissing her forehead, and then he lit two cigarettes and handed her one, and she inhaled deeply, the nicotine calming he down.

"Can you stay tonight?" she asked hopefully, and he smiled and reassured her, telling her "Yes, and tomorrow night as well."

"But what about your wife, who's going to look after her?" Violet asked anxiously. "Won't she wonder where you are?"

"It's okay, she has a full-time carer now," Harry soothed her, "and I told her I was going to a fashion convention to look at some new designs. She's not expecting me back till Monday."

"That's good," Violet said, and sighed contentedly. She stubbed out the cigarette and snuggled up to him and he said, "In the morning I'll give you breakfast in bed, the full English."

Violet raised an eyebrow and slid a questing hand under the quilt. "Mm, the full English, sounds promising, but why wait until morning?" and switched off the light.

Chapter 3

Doreen would have liked to have spent a lot longer at Honeysuckle Cottage on her first visit in order to learn more about her Aunt May, but Raymond's impatience meant that she had to try and glean some information from the handful of correspondence that she had found in her aunt's wardrobe. Relations between Violet and her daughter had been strained ever since Doreen had brought home May's letters. Violet had demanded to see them, but Doreen, fearing that her mother would most probably tear them up, had refused, for she was determined to get to the bottom of the mystery.

When she had read through them all, Doreen thought she had at last found out the reason for the feud between her aunt and her mother, and it had to do with her father, James Bland. She had been surprised to find a letter to May written by her father from France, and dated two weeks before his death. Rather poignantly it contained a pressed flower, and he had written:-

My Darling May,

I think of you every waking minute. You can't imagine the hell of his place, but yesterday, among all the mud, I found this wild rose that was struggling to bloom, and it touched my heart. You will always be my wild flower of the woods, and I send it to you with my love, in the hope that you will someday forgive me.

Your loving James.

May's heart had leapt when she recognised James' handwriting on the envelope, and she was surprised and touched to read his note and to realise that he still loved her. She had not been able to forget him, and a small glimmer of hope appeared that maybe, once the war was over, he would come back to her. She had, after a lot of heart searching, eventually managed to forgive him and had kept in touch with his mother who kept her informed with all the news, but soon her hopes were to be cruelly dashed.

James had taken advantage of a few hours respite from the battle to write letters to his mother and to Violet, and on impulse he sent the rose to May. She had been constantly in his thoughts, and he longed for the hellish war to end and to be able to return home. He had made up his mind that he would go and see May the next time that he could get home on leave, and perhaps she would at last be able to forgive him.

He knew that he had been careless in getting Violet pregnant, and he felt guilty because he didn't love her, but he knew that she loved him. He adored his little daughter though, and wouldn't be without her now, and he tenderly kissed her photo and put it safely back in his pocket. He looked around with compassion at his men; they were all in the same boat, as all were filthy dirty, bone weary and very homesick, and each one of them was terrified.

The following day they were ordered to push the lines forward, but as James led his men onward he stepped on a landmine that blew off both his legs. As he lay with his face half-buried in mud he found it strange that he could feel no pain, but as the life blood pumped out of him he thought he could see the figure of a woman that appeared to hover in front of him. At first he thought it was May, and he tried to call her name, but then he saw that it was his grandmother. She was bathed in light and looked young and lovely again, just as she looked in the photograph on his mother's desk, and she had come to take him home.

Doreen was puzzled, for she had been three years old when her father was killed. When had he been seeing May, and what was there to forgive? Among the letters was a photograph of her father with his arm round May, and they looked very happy, but there was no clue to the date. Her father was not in uniform, so had the picture been taken before the war or when he was home on leave? Doreen also found several letters from her mother. There was a card to inform her aunt of the birth of a daughter, the 3rd of April, 1939, Doreen May, weighing 6lb 12 oz. and a letter to inform May of the death in action of her father James, and then a letter that had her guessing. It was dated 1943, and said:-

Dear May,

I came to see you in hospital several times, but you were so out of it that I don't suppose you even knew I was there. I'm so, so sorry for what happened, you were so brave, and I don't think I could have done what you did. Mother was terribly upset, but at least you're alive, and that's something to be thankful for.

Doreen has become a right little handful and keeps me on the go from morning till night. She's a pretty little thing and takes after you in looks, but with James' colouring, and I will send you a photo for Christmas. I do hope and pray that you get better very soon, and once again I am so sorry for everything.

Your loving sister, Violet.

Her mother had never mentioned that May had spent a time in hospital, so Doreen surmised that maybe the reason she had never been allowed to see her aunt was because she was an invalid, too sick to have visitors. Doreen reflected sadly that her aunt would most probably have been rather lonely, and perhaps if she had been allowed to visit she could have somehow found a way to heal the rift between Violet and her sister. There was one final letter, dated June 1948, when she was nine years old:-

Dear May,

Thank you for your invitation to have Doreen to stay, but I don't really think it's a good idea, do you? I know you mean well, but I think the poor child would be frightened to death, so I think it's best just to exchange letters for the time being. I enclose her latest school photo and I'm pleased to say that she is doing very well in her lessons, much better than I ever did, so she takes after you in more ways than one.

Look after yourself, Violet.

The mystery deepened, and Doreen realised that her Aunt May had really wanted her to come for a visit, and she had certainly kept all her letters and photographs, but then why had her mother always told her that her aunt was a recluse who didn't want to be around people? And why would she have been frightened? Was her aunt mentally ill and perhaps prone to violence? She needed to get to the truth of the matter, and was determined to confront her mother as soon as she got home from work.

Violet kicked off her shoes as soon as got in and said, "Make us a cuppa, there's a pet."

Doreen dutifully put the kettle on, then said, "I've been reading through those letters I found at Aunty May's, and I think I know why you and her weren't speaking." Violet went a bit pale, but said nothing, so Doreen continued. "She and Daddy were having an affair, weren't they? And that's why you couldn't forgive her."

Violet gave a bitter laugh and said, "So that's what you think, is it? Well you couldn't be more wrong."

"But I don't understand, there's a picture of Daddy with his arm round her, and he's not in uniform, and then there's a letter from France." Now it was Violet's turn to be surprised, and she turned to Doreen and said sharply, "From France? Show me."

"No," retorted Doreen stubbornly, "not till I find out the truth."

Violet sighed and said with resignation, "Well, I guess you're old enough to understand," and she began to tell Doreen her story.

Chapter 4

May Turner had been walking out with James Bland for almost a year, and everyone was saying it was high time they got engaged. He eventually proposed just before her eighteenth birthday, and they'd had their photo taken in a professional studio to mark the event. Now, as they walked home after church, he had pulled her into a secluded place behind the churchyard wall and attempted to make love to her. "Don't do that, James, please. You know I want to wait until we're married," she had said firmly.

He had replied with frustration, "Oh May, you really know how to make a chap suffer. You know I'm crazy about you."

It was no good, no matter how many times he tried May refused to give in, insisting on saving herself for their wedding night. James adored May who, with her full breasts and long chestnut hair worn in a chignon, was his ideal woman, but he was growing increasingly frustrated by her refusal to let him make love to her. She was inclined to be rather serious and strait-laced in her outlook, whereas her younger sister, Violet, was far more flighty. She was taller and more willowy than May, with a fashionably boyish figure and her fair curls shorn in a bob, and she was also far more frivolous and light-hearted in her demeanour.

One evening, after he had seen May home, he heard a giggle and, looking up, saw her sister peering down at him from a tree. "Have you been spying on us?" he asked with mock severity, and she jumped down lightly and grinned cheekily at him.

"And what if I have? There was nothing to see with Saint May anyway."

"Well, you're a very naughty girl, and do you know what happens to naughty girls?"

"Ooh, do tell!" giggled Violet, and he thought to himself, *My God, she's become a right little beauty!*

Out loud he said, "They get smacked bottoms," and gave her a hard slap on her rump and then added "and your sister May isn't quite as prim and proper as you think."

That night in bed Violet asked curiously, "May, have you and James, you know, done it yet?"

"Certainly not," replied May indignantly, "you know I'm saving myself for our wedding night."

"What do you get up to with James then?"

"That's none of your business," she replied tartly.

"I bet he's enormous, isn't he?" she giggled, but May refused to reply other than to tell her to shut up and go to sleep, and Violet sighed and turned over and cuddled her pillow, pretending that it was James she was holding.

The next time he saw Violet was in church, and she looked at him slyly and smiled, and when he had walked May home, he found that she was waiting for him at the bottom of the lane, and she called out to him "Hello James, where are you off to now?"

"To the pub for a drink," he said curtly.

"Can I come with you?" she beseeched.

He retorted "Don't be silly Violet, for one thing you're not old enough."

"I'm nearly seventeen," she said indignantly.

He grinned down at her and said teasingly, "Sweet sixteen, and never been kissed?" and when she didn't reply he bent and kissed her hard on the lips.

She looked startled for a moment and then asked, "Is that how you kiss May?" He shook his head, and she said, "Show me, kiss me the way you do May." He kissed her again, a slow lingering kiss, slipping his tongue into her mouth, and she went weak at the knees and clung to him. He touched her breasts, which were not as full as May's but small and firm, and as he slipped a hand inside her blouse, he realised she was naked beneath the thin cotton.

Her skin was warm and silky smooth, her nipple a hard little bud against his hand, and suddenly he could not control himself any longer but pulled her to the ground at the base of an old tree and took her quickly. She gave a little cry of pain as he entered her, but this soon changed to moans of pleasure, and when he was spent, she sighed and said, "That was wonderful James. May doesn't know what she's missing."

James leaned back against the tree and lit up a cigarette. "You mustn't say anything to May," he said earnestly, "it would break her heart; this is our secret, promise?"

"I promise," said Violet archly, "but only if you give me a ciggy."

"You don't smoke, do you?" James asked in surprise.

Violet giggled and said, "No, but I can learn."

"Alright then," James said and lit one for her, and she took a puff and immediately began to cough and splutter. He grinned and said, "Serves you right!" but she was determined not to be beaten and was going to finish the cigarette if it killed her.

Violet had thoroughly enjoyed her first sexual experience and wanted to do it again, and so each Sunday, after church, when he had walked May home, she waited for him at the bottom of the lane. James too, looked forward to their weekly encounters, as Violet was keen and eager to learn, but he wished it could have been May, as he felt that she was always withholding a part of herself, and he longed for her to love him with the same abandon that her sister did.

He knew they were playing a dangerous game, and although generally he was careful, once they had almost been caught when they heard Jed approaching. He was whistling tunelessly, but then stopped when he spotted Violet in the shrubbery and asked "What'm you up to in there?"

"Nothing," she giggled and blushed, and then laughed, "Trust you to spot me when I've been caught short."

"Don't worry, I didn't see nothing," he reassured her.

She emerged, straightening her dress, and took his arm and asked "Have you been fishing?"

Jed nodded, "Aye, but I've had no luck today," and as they disappeared along the path James emerged and breathed a sigh of relief.

One day, however, when he was meeting with Violet, she was not her usual coquettish self, but quiet and withdrawn, and when James asked her what was wrong, she burst into tears and sobbed, "I'm pregnant!"

"Are you quite sure?" asked James.

She retorted angrily, "Of course I'm sure! What are we going to do now?"

"I don't know, let me think," he muttered and paced up and down while Violet sat quietly and waited for his decision. At last he said, "We'll have to tell May, and then perhaps, once we're married, you could come and stay with us till the baby's born. We could bring it up as our own, and no-one need be any the wiser."

Violet was taken aback as she had expected him to propose marriage to her, but he was still firmly set on marrying May. "Do you think she'd agree to that?" asked Violet doubtfully.

James retorted "I don't know, but it seems the best solution to me."

They decided to tell May the following Sunday after church, and both Violet and James were dreading the ordeal. In the kitchen of Honeysuckle Cottage Mrs Turner was getting the tea ready and as they entered James cleared his throat tentatively. "Mrs Turner, May, I'm afraid I've got something rather upsetting to tell you." Violet sat quietly in the corner, wishing the floor would open up and swallow her, as James continued haltingly. "I... I'm afraid I've done something rather foolish... I've got Violet in the family way."

"Oh!" May gasped and turned ashen.

Mrs Turner shouted, "Quick, catch her!" as May keeled over, and James sprang over and caught her just before she crashed to the floor.

When she came round, Mrs Turner helped her to sit at the kitchen table and handed her a glass of water, and she was white and trembling, but her voice was firm as she asked James, "How could you do this to me?"

"I'm so, so sorry May, I never meant to hurt you, but I'm only human, and you never let me..."

"Don't you dare lay this at my door!" shouted May furiously, "you could have shown some self control, and why did you choose my sister, of all people?"

"It wasn't meant to happen," he protested lamely "it just did, I'm so sorry."

"And as for you..." May turned angrily to Violet, "how could you betray me, haven't I always been good to you?"

"May, please don't," Violet sobbed. "I'm truly sorry for hurting you, but I love James too."

"But he was MINE! We were betrothed; didn't that mean anything to you?"

Violet hid her face in her hands and sobbed uncontrollably, but James said calmly, "May, look, it's not the end of the world. We can still get married, and then Violet could come and stay and we could look after her baby and..."

"Are you mad? Do you think I want to marry you after this? I never want to see the pair of you again as long as I live!" And with that she ran upstairs, slamming the bedroom door behind her and, throwing herself on her bed, cried her heart out.

Mrs Turner turned to James and said coldly "You and Violet had best get wed as soon as possible, and then move right away from here. I don't want May upset by seeing you around the village with your baby." To Violet she said, "Stop your bawling, you've got what you wanted, even though it meant breaking May's heart. Now, get out of my sight, the pair of you."

When May had calmed down somewhat she thought over what James had proposed, but he really had no idea what he was asking of her. Her sister Violet had always got her own way ever since she was little, and in order to keep the peace May always had been made to give in to her. If May had a new doll, then Violet wanted to play with it, and although she would eventually get it back, it would be damaged in some way, or she would borrow May's new blouse without asking, and then return it indelibly stained or with a button missing. Whatever May had, Violet wanted, and now she had stolen the love of her life and she would never, ever forgive her.

James and Violet were married six weeks later in a registry office, and they moved away to live with James' grandfather. When Doreen was born Violet sent May a card, but if she had hoped for a reconciliation she was to be disappointed, for neither May nor her mother wrote back.

Chapter 5

May had first met James the previous summer. She had been waiting at the bus-stop precariously balancing a pile of library books and a paper bag containing her sister's shoes that needed repairing, when a small black Ford had pulled up and a young man wound down the passenger side window. Thinking he needed directions, she bent forward, dropping some of the books in the process, but he said, "If you're waiting for the bus, I'm afraid you've missed it, it's already gone."

"Oh no," sighed May, "it must have been early. What time do you make it?"

"Ten past two." She looked at her watch and grimaced, saying "Oh bother, my watch is running slow again."

He had jumped out of the car and bent to retrieve her books, saying "If you're going into Upper Bulford I could give you a lift. I'm going that way myself, and it wold be no trouble."

"I don't usually accept lifts from strange men," May said politely, "but thanks for the offer."

He grinned down at her, and she was aware of a pair of the brightest blue eyes she had ever seen. "I'm not really a stranger," he countered, "I think you must know my mother, she's a teacher at the local school, Mrs Bland."

"Oh, then you must be…"

"James Bland at your service." He laughed, giving a little bow, and then asked "Now then, how about that lift?"

"Alright then, thank you," May smiled. "I do need to get to the library as Mum frets if she doesn't have anything to read."

James opened the door, and taking the books from her, threw them carelessly on to the back seat. He had noticed May in church a couple of times and had been struck by how lovely she was, and now he had the opportunity to find out more about her.

"Your mother said you were at university, are you home on leave?" May asked him.

"No, I've finished my studies and I've got my degree now," he replied.

"So you'll be staying around here then?" she asked hopefully.

He grinned and said, "Well, that all depends."

"Depends on what?"

"On whether I get the job at the bank or not."

"Is that where you're going now," asked May, "to an interview?"

"Yes, but what about you? Do you have a job?"

"Sort of," replied May, pulling a face. "I'm filling in for my mother at present as housemaid up at the manor. She's not been very well since my father died, and someone has to earn some money, but I'm hoping to go to teacher's training college next year. Your mother has always been very encouraging, but until Mum's feeling better there's no chance."

"I'm sorry to hear that," said James sincerely. "I think you'd make a very good teacher."

"What makes you think that?" asked May curiously.

He thought a moment and then replied with a smile "Well, you have a calm presence, a kind heart and an enquiring mind."

"And you gleaned all that from our brief conversation?" laughed May. "But what if I couldn't control a class of children? I'd be a hopeless teacher then."

"You'd have no trouble with the children," James grinned, "they'd probably do anything you asked them just to win your approval."

May blushed and fell silent, and soon they were on the outskirts of town and James asked, "Shall I drop you by the library?" She nodded, and he pulled up outside and then jumped out to open the car door for her. He retrieved the books from the back seat and handed them to her, saying "Look, why don't we meet at the Tudor tea-rooms in an hour, and you can either help me celebrate or commiserate with me?"

"That would be very nice," replied May, impressed by his good manners, and she wished him luck before he drove off with a cheery wave.

May was a little late arriving at the tea-rooms as it had taken longer than she had anticipated to get everything done, and she saw that James was already there, anxiously watching the door, but he relaxed and smiled when he saw her. She was flushed pink from hurrying, and apologised for keeping him waiting, but he said, "I'm just glad you're here, because I wasn't at all sure if you'd turn up."

She was surprised that he wasn't quite as confident as he'd first appeared, but she sat down and asked how his interview went.

"I got the job," he told her triumphantly, "and I start on Monday."

"That's wonderful news," May cried, "your mother will be thrilled."

James' father had been killed in the First World War, and then it had just been him and his mother, and she had doted on her only son, so he said, "Yes, she was a bit lonely while I was away at university, so it'll be nice for her to have some company again."

He had taken the liberty of ordering a pot of tea and a plate of fresh cream cakes, but as he offered it to May she looked rueful and said, "I'm not sure I should be eating cream cakes, they're rather fattening, and I have to watch my figure."

"What's wrong with your figure?" asked James, "it looks perfectly lovely to me." May blushed and for a moment didn't know what to say, and then they both started to speak at the same time which made them laugh, and James said, "I was going to ask you if you'd like to come for tea one Sunday, as I'm sure my mother would like to see you."

"This Sunday?" asked May.

James nodded, "Yes, but I'll have to check with her first, although I'm sure it will be fine. I'll pick you up at four o'clock."

When he had dropped her off at her home May ran in, handed her mother the books and said excitedly "Guess what? James Bland has asked me round to tea on Sunday!"

"Well, there's a thing!" exclaimed Mrs Turner. "Whatever are you going to wear?"

"My blue dress I suppose; I was going to alter it anyway as I've bought some lace to sew on it, and if I could borrow your pearls, then I think it will do perfectly well."

"Of course you can borrow my pearls, and I'm glad you've met a nice young man at last. Teacher's son, isn't he?"

"Yes, and he's polite and charming and so handsome!"

"And clever too, not like that ignoramus Jed Fuller that's always hanging round you."

"Oh Jed's just a friend."

"I think he'd like to be more than a friend," chuckled her mother. "He can hardly take his eyes off you."

"Oh Mum," May reassured her, "you really don't have to worry about Jed."

On Sunday May waited impatiently for the morning service to be over so that she could go home and get ready for her date. She had waved to Mrs Bland in church, and after the service she had confirmed that James would be picking her up at four, and so May had dashed home to wash her hair, and to brush it dry in front of the range before changing into her dress. James arrived promptly and whistled appreciatively when he saw her. "I say, you look a real picture in that dress, is it new?"

"No, but I'm glad you like it. I'm feeling a bit nervous though," confessed May.

James reassured her, saying "There's really no need. Mother's so looking forward to seeing you again. Didn't you know, you used to be her star pupil?"

Mrs Bland greeted May with a kiss and said warmly "Welcome my dear, it's nice to see you again, come on through." She led the way to the rear of the house saying, "I thought we'd have tea in the garden as it's such a lovely afternoon. I do hope you like salmon?"

"Yes thank you," said May and handed her a bunch of flowers picked from the garden of Honeysuckle Cottage.

"Oh how lovely, such gorgeous roses," cried Mrs Bland and sniffed appreciatively, and while she went to put them in water James showed May out on to the terrace.

A small table had been covered with a starched, embroidered cloth and a plate of tinned salmon took pride of place in the centre, together with a bowl of potato salad and some dainty triangular cucumber sandwiches with the crusts cut off. On a separate wooden cake-stand was a Victoria sponge and some iced cupcakes, and May exclaimed "Oh you've gone to so much trouble Mrs Bland, and it all looks lovely."

"I thought we could have little glass of wine to celebrate James' new job at the bank," said Mrs Bland. "Would you do the honours dear?" she handed him the bottle and the corkscrew and then asked "And how is your poor mother May? Any sign of improvement?"

"Not really," sighed May, "she has her good days, but I'm afraid she's not really up to going back to work just yet."

"It's such a shame you had to postpone your career. Still, perhaps by next year…?"

She looked quizzically at May who nodded and said, "Hopefully, as Violet will have left school by then and could take over at the manor if Mum is still unwell, and then perhaps I can go to teacher's training college after all."

May sipped her wine slowly. It tasted like vinegar to her, but she enjoyed the salmon, which was a rare treat for her, and the cakes that Mrs Bland served with a pot of Earl Grey tea. James had been rather quiet but now, after the second glass of wine, he became more expansive and began to regale them with stories of his university days to make them laugh.

At seven May thanked James' mother and said she would have to go, but offered to help with the washing-up. "Nonsense dear," she replied, "James will run you home, and I hope you'll come again soon."

Before they reached the house James asked "Do you really have to go in yet?"

May nodded and said, "I'm afraid so, as I have to get Mum some supper and see that Violet's clothes are ready for school tomorrow."

"Well then, would you like to come to the cinema with me on Friday? I think there's a new Fred Astaire film showing at the Gaumont."

May couldn't remember the last time she'd been to the cinema, so she smiled and said delightedly "Yes, that would be lovely."

At the gate of Honeysuckle Cottage James opened the car door for May and walked her to the front door, but as she turned to say goodnight he suddenly bent and kissed her full on the lips. It took her breath away, and she blushed, and James grinned and said, "I'll pick you up at six o'clock on Friday."

Violet was waiting for her in the kitchen and asked eagerly "Well, did he kiss you?"

May smiled, and blushing a little, said, "Yes, actually, he did."

"And how was it?"

"Lovely, not that it's any of your business."

"So are you seeing him again?"

"Yes, he's going to take me to the cinema on Friday," May told her.

Violet sighed and said enviously "You are so lucky. I wish I had someone nice to take me out."

Her mother countered "Don't even think about it my girl, you're far too young to go out with boys."

Chapter 6

On their first date to the cinema James was the perfect gentleman, but the second time he had taken her out he made sure that they sat in the back row, and then he had kissed her and tried to touch her breasts beneath her sweater. "Don't, someone might see," May had admonished him, but he assured her that everyone's eyes would be glued to the screen, and then he had begun to caress her knee, letting his hand stray to the smooth skin at the top of her stocking, but she would let him go no further.

They began to go out on a regular basis, usually to the cinema, but sometimes just going for walks or to watch the local cricket team play. One evening he drove them to a secluded place and parked the car where they could not be seen, and then he began to kiss May passionately and undid her bra so that he could caress her full breasts. At first she was embarrassed and wondered whether he should be doing that, and pushed him away, but he reassured her saying, "It isn't wrong May, it's normal for two people who care for each other." It did give her a thrill of pleasure that went straight to the secret place between her thighs, and when his hand caressed her there she did not want him to stop.

After a while he unbuttoned his flies and took her hand and placed it there. She was unsure what he wanted of her, and when she asked him he sighed and said, "God, you are such an innocent. Do you really not know what to do?" She shook her head, and then he guided her hand to his shaft and said, "Move it up and down for a bit, please May."

"Like this?" she asked, rubbing her hand gently along its length, but he exhorted her to do it harder, and then his breathing quickened and he gave a little groan, and she stopped and asked nervously "Did I hurt you?"

"No, no, please don't stop," he begged, and at last he came into her hand, and taking out his handkerchief, he wiped the stickiness from her fingers. It was May's first experience of being with a man, and she had no friends to confide in, no-one to tell her if what she was doing was right or wrong. The only friend from school that she could have asked had moved away, and her mother had always told her that giving in to men would make them disrespect her. At first she worried that she had cheapened herself, but James had enjoyed it and it seemed that he had not lost his respect for her after all. She therefore came to the conclusion that this was how all lovers behaved and, as long as she kept her virginity, it was fine to do what he wanted.

James drove to their secluded place at least once a week to repeat their petting sessions, and she began to look forward to their time alone together, and although she was still very shy, it all took place in the dark and somehow that made it alright, and she began to long for the thrill that his experienced fingers gave her. She steadfastly refused to let him go all the way however, and still could not believe her luck that someone so good looking and well-educated would fall for a simple country girl like her. He was her first real love, and she was deliriously happy.

When James' bank held their centennial celebrations he invited May to the ball, and it was her first formal occasion and she was excited, but also a little nervous about letting him down in front of his employers. "I've got nothing smart, so what on earth shall I wear Mum?" she asked her mother in despair.

Mrs Turner thought a moment and then said, "There's no money to buy you a new frock, but I'll come up to the manor with you tomorrow and speak to Elsie. Perhaps she could find you an old gown to borrow that had belonged to the mistress."

Mrs Turner was as good as her word, and got up early to accompany May to her job at Bulford Manor, where her old friend Elsie was the housekeeper. She was delighted to see Mrs Turner again, and invited her into her private parlour for a cup of tea and a good gossip, and when her friend explained that May had been invited to a grand ball but had nothing to wear, Elsie said she would see what she could do.

Later, when May had finished her duties, Elsie slipped her a brown paper package and told her it had belonged to the mistress, who wouldn't miss it, and to hide it under her coat. When she got home she unwrapped the parcel and was thrilled to find a beautiful oyster-coloured, long silk dress trimmed with clusters of seed pearls, and with a few judicious nips and tucks, it fitted her perfectly.

On the eve of the ball May borrowed her mother's pearl necklace and earrings to set off the gown and Mrs Turner looked at her proudly and said, "You look a picture May, I only wish that your father could have seen you." James was very complimentary too, but seemed unaccountably nervous, and May thought it was because he was worried about showing himself up on the dance floor, but he was a competent dancer, and May thoroughly enjoyed the evening.

At the end of the final dance he suddenly produced a small box containing a simple diamond ring and asked her "May, would you do me the honour of becoming my wife?" She had secretly nursed a hope that he would propose, and it explained his nervousness, so she did not keep him waiting but without hesitation said yes.

Mrs Turner was delighted at the news, and Violet was green with envy. "You lucky thing May," she had cried "you've bagged the best looking man in the county, and look at the size of that diamond!"

When Mrs Bland heard the news she couldn't have been happier and welcomed May with a kiss, saying "My dear, I'm so pleased you're marrying James, and I think you'll make him a wonderful wife. Don't give up on going to teacher's training college though, as I know James wouldn't prevent you from following your dream, and I'll give you all the help I can."

Jed, however, was upset at May's news, and when she showed him her engagement ring he begged her to reconsider. "He ain't no good for you May, he's a right gad about and he'll end up breaking your heart."

"You're just jealous Jed, "May chided him. "James is very kind and he truly loves me."

"Well I reckon he ain't no husband material. Look, I knows I can't read nor write, but I'd work damn hard and I'd always be true to you May, so marry me instead. What about it?"

"No Jed, you're my dearest friend, but I'm afraid that's all you'll ever be."

He begged her for one kiss before parting, and because he looked so hang-dog she felt sorry for him and agreed. He watched her walk away with a heavy heart, but then, after a while, realising that he would never have a chance with her, he turned his attentions to Nellie, the milkman's daughter. When she fell pregnant he did the decent thing and married her, but May would always be his first love, and he would always remain he true friend.

James was very keen to have the marriage as soon as possible because May would not sleep with him until after the wedding ring was on her finger. She was very proper about such things, and would have found it mortifying to be pregnant before the wedding. James was saving hard to put a deposit on a house, and May meanwhile was busy embroidering tablecloths and cushion covers for her bottom drawer, and saving what she could from her meagre wages for some new underwear and nightgowns.

Mrs Bland had kindly offered to let them live with her after the wedding until they could afford a place of their own, and looked forward to having May as a daughter-in-law, so it came as a terrible shock when James had to confess to her that he had got May's sister Violet pregnant, and would have to marry her instead. "But how could you James?" his mother had cried. "Poor, poor May, she's such a lovely girl and she didn't deserve to be doubly betrayed like that."

James felt very bad about it, he'd been selfish and careless, but the deed was done now and there was nothing he could do to make things better. He brought Violet round to meet his mother the following day, as Mrs Turner had thrown her out and she had nowhere else to go, but Mrs Bland simply could not warm to her. It wasn't just that she had betrayed May, but she thought her a self-centred and shallow young woman who only thought about her own amusement.

James and Violet were married six weeks later in a registry office in Upper Bulford, but neither May nor her mother came to the wedding. Immediately after the ceremony they move away to live with James' paternal grandfather as Violet had felt uncomfortable living under the same roof as her mother-in-law, who had made her feelings quite clear. The old man lived in the suburbs of London, and was glad to welcome the young couple, and when Doreen was born he was delighted to have a great-grandchild to spoil. Violet sent May a card to inform her of the birth, but if she had hoped for a reconciliation she was to be disappointed, for neither May nor her mother wrote back.

Chapter 7

Doreen had been quite shocked by her mother's revelations and said, "Poor Aunty May, she must have been devastated. How could you do that to your own sister?"

"Well I didn't intend to, did I?" said Violet ruefully, "but your father was a very attractive man. He had real class and was so handsome, and with his auburn hair he was just like a red setter among a bunch of mongrels, and it wasn't easy to say no to him. If I hadn't got pregnant he would have married May, and no-one would have been any the wiser. You should know how easy it is to make a mistake," and she gestured at Doreen's growing belly. "Now, show me the letter please."

Doreen handed it over, and her mother read it, her mouth compressed into a thin line. She had always suspected that James still had feelings for May, but it was no less of a shock to have them confirmed. It had hurt Violet deeply in those early months of their marriage to realise that James was still in love with May. It was like a knife thrust to her heart, and even after all these years she still could not forget him, for he had been the love of her life.

She had loved him with a fierce passion and although she loved Harry Marvel, it was a different kind of love. They had been two lonely souls coming together, comfort sought and comfort given, and though Harry clearly adored her, she would have traded in every minute spent with him for one more day together with James.

Violet hadn't wanted him to join the army at the beginning of the war, begging him to wait until he was called up, but James had felt that it was his duty and she could not make him change his mind. His own father had been killed in the First World War and he wanted to honour his memory, and because he had been to university it was felt that he was prime officer material. James' grandfather was not in the best of health, and as well as having a young child to look after, Violet also had to take care of him, a job she found arduous as she was not cut out for being a nurse. When James was killed in action the shock and grief finished off his old grandfather, and he passed away not long after, leaving her to cope entirely on her own with not a soul she could turn to for support.

Violet was very short of money after the old man died, and to make ends meet she put an advertisement in the newsagent's window that she had a room to let, and it was Rita who came to see it the very next day. She was a couple of years older than Violet and worked as a waitress at the Lyons Corner House, but they had hit it off immediately and became the best of friends, so when May had her accident and was in hospital, she offered to take time off to look after Doreen.

Rita like to have a good time, and encouraged Violet to go dancing, frequently persuading her mother to come round to baby-sit little Doreen so that she could take her to a place she knew that was full of G.I. soldiers. Consequently, they were never short of nylons and chocolate, but Violet could not forget James and turned down the many offers to go out on dates that she received.

She now fished out the photo of him that she always carried in her handbag. He looked so handsome in his uniform, tall and with chiselled features, and she tried to imagine how he would have looked now. She thought he would have aged well, and would probably have been even better looking with a few laugh lines and a touch of grey in his auburn hair. Well, it was no good crying over spilt milk, and with a sigh she put the photo back in her bag and closed it with a snap. Then she did what she always did when she was upset; she got out the bottle of Brasso and a duster and began to polish the fender as if her life depended on it.

When she had finished Doreen asked her why she had never let her visit with her Aunt May and said accusingly "You told me she didn't like to be around people but that was a lie, wasn't it? She wanted me to come and stay."

"I know she did," sighed her mother, "but you remember what I told you about her heroism?"

"Yes, you said she rescued some boys from a fire."

"Well, what I didn't tell you was that she had been horribly burnt; she looked a fright."

"Oh poor Aunt May." Doreen was overcome with pity for her aunt, imagining her loneliness, and her eyes brimmed with tears and she said, "How awful."

"Yes, it was truly awful," agreed Violet, "but I was only trying to protect you. You would have had nightmares for weeks; I know I did when I saw her in hospital."

"You should have told me sooner," Doreen cried angrily, "then I could have made up my own mind, but it's too bloody late now, isn't it?"

"Yes, I'm sorry dear," Violet sighed. "I was going to tell you eventually, but I didn't know May was going to die so soon, did I?"

When Violet had left with James, May continued to live at Honeysuckle Cottage with her mother. Their father had been a forester, working on the Bulford estate, and the cottage had been tied to the job. When Mr Turner died, Squire Bulford had let them live at the cottage until he needed it for a replacement forester, but he had not managed to find anyone. May's mother had been employed as a maid at the manor, but since her husband's death she suffered from depression, and had not been able to work. Mr Turner had died out in the woods, felled like one of his trees by a massive stroke, which killed him outright. He had been a simple man who had never learnt to read and write, but his wife was literate and made sure that their daughter's education was as good, if not better, than her own.

May was the bookish one, with hopes of becoming a school teacher, but her father's death and her mother's consequent debilitation, meant that she had to leave school and find work. She took over her mother's job of housemaid at the manor, and became the family's sole breadwinner. Her mother's depression worsened once Violet had left, and she took no interest in her surroundings, and sometimes took to her bed for days at a time.

May felt very isolated, and although she hated her sister, she missed her company and having someone to talk to, and lying in bed alone at night she would torture herself with images of James and Violet together, and to bring comfort, would touch herself and pretend that it was his fingers that were giving her pleasure. She swore that she would never forgive her sister for stealing James away from her and confining her to a life of unremitting drudgery.

In 1939 war broke out, and James was called up to fight, as were the Squire's sons, and the nation was urged to dig for victory and May and her mother turned the whole of their garden over to growing vegetables. Her mother seemed to benefit from being out in the fresh air and having something to focus on, and for a time they rubbed along comfortably. Then, in 1942 May received two letters. The first was from James to tell her how much he missed her, how miserable he was, and that he still loved her.

He had made up his mind that if he should survive the war, then he would go back to May and beg her forgiveness and ask her to take him back. He had never really loved Violet, although he thought the world of his little daughter, but he would leave her well provided for, and Violet would soon find someone else. The horror of the battle going on all round him and the men he had seen die made him realise that life was precious and one had to make the most of it, and he loved May with all his heart and could not get her out of his thoughts.

That letter from James gave May hope that perhaps, when war was over, he would divorce Violet and come back to marry her, but when she received the second letter her hopes were cruelly dashed. It was from Violet; to inform her that James had been killed in action.

May carried on with her daily life, but her heart was heavy. She would have liked to join the WACS, anything to get away, but she couldn't leave her mother. One morning, as she trudged to work at the manor, she smelled smoke and, rounding the corner, saw that the barn was on fire. She started to run and, to her horror, saw Squire Bulford's grandsons trapped in the hayloft. "Help us!! Please help us!" they screamed, and without a qualm May ran into the barn and scrambled up the ladder to the loft. The hay was well ablaze, and the smoke was choking her, but she grabbed Peter, the youngest boy, and covering his face with her scarf, started to descend the ladder with him clinging to her neck. He was crying and coughing, and once he was safely out of the barn, she dunked her coat in the cattle trough, wrapped it round her head, and climbed back up to rescue Stephen.

By this time everybody had come running towards the barn, and she could hear the clang of the fire engine in the distance, but the flames were now so high that escape down the ladder was impossible. With her heart pounding she looked round in desperation, and then saw a length of rope. Somehow she managed to tie it securely round Stephen's waist, and then lowered him out of the window to the arms of the waiting crowd. The thick smoke was beginning to fill her lungs, choking her until she could barely catch her breath, and she feared that she was going to pass out. She was terrified as she could feel the almost unbearable heat radiating through the wooden floor, and her feet were beginning to blister through the thin soles of her shoes.

Flames started to lick through the cracks of the floorboards and she began to scream in panic, and Jed shouted up to her "For God's sake, jump May, we'll catch you!" She looked down at their upturned, expectant faces waiting below, but she had always been afraid of heights, and the cobbled courtyard looked such a long way down. "I... I can't," she cried, but then to her relief she saw the fire engine had arrived and the men were running towards her with the ladder, but just before they could reach her, the floor gave way and she fell down into the blazing inferno.

When they pulled her out of the burning building, the whole left side of her body was blackened, with her hair and clothes burnt off, but she was still alive. Just. For three days it was touch and go if she would live or die, her mother never leaving her side, but then she began to regain consciousness, and it seemed as if she would survive.

When her mother first saw May she did not recognise her, and so horrific were the burns that she prayed for her to die. She sent a telegram to Violet, who came as soon as she could get someone to look after Doreen, and then her best friend Rita offered to look after the little girl while she went to give her mother her support. Violet wept in her mother's arms when she saw May, and cried "I can't bear to see her like that, she doesn't look like herself any more. Poor, poor May, I just want to make amends, is there anything I can do?"

Her mother shrugged hopelessly, "I don't see what you can do, 'cept pray, that's all any of us can do at the moment." She visited as often as she could, but Rita needed to get back to work, so it was not possible to leave her little girl for any length of time.

It was a long, slow road to recovery, but eventually May was well enough to leave the hospital. She had not been allowed any mirrors, but now the moment of truth had been reached, and May had to come to terms with her injuries. When she saw her face for the first time she uttered a piercing scream and cried piteously, "No! No, I can't bear it; you should have let me die!" Nothing the nurses or her mother could say would comfort her, for her face was more hideous than any Halloween mask.

The whole left side of her face was red and puckered, pulling the corner of her mouth up into a snarl. Her left eye was blind and scarred, her ear melted into a shapeless lump, and half her hair had been burnt away. The doctors had also been forced to amputate her left hand, leaving a stump that ended just below the elbow. Her life was over at twenty-two years of age, for what man would ever look at her now, and if she found the sight of herself so repulsive, how much worse for people who did not know her?

When she had been back at Honeysuckle Cottage for about three weeks, she had a visit from Squire Bulford. She could see he was shocked and repelled by her injuries, for he could not look her in the eye, but he thanked her from the bottom of his heart for saving the lives of his grandsons, and he told May she could stay in the cottage for the rest of her life, and he would provide a small allowance for her and her mother to live on.

The only other visitor to come to Honeysuckle cottage was her old school friend Jed Fuller who had been in love with May. He was employed as a gardener up at the manor, and the Squire had pulled a few strings to avoid his being called up because he provided vital war work on the land, growing crops to feed the nation. With the lack of available labour, he was also called on to do a bit of hedging and ditching, coppicing and fencing, and indeed any odd jobs that needed doing, and yet he always managed to find time to supply May and her mother with a few vegetables or the odd rabbit for the pot.

With the approach of winter he brought the Turners a load of logs for their fire and, as he entered the kitchen, May ran upstairs and hid. "May," he called, "it's me, Jed, you remember me from school, don't you?"

"Yes, and thank you for the logs," she called down, "now please go away."

It was dark on the staircase, and he could only see the shape of her, but he called back "Come down May, don't be ashamed of how you look, you'm a bloody heroine."

Tentatively she crept down the stairs, hanging back in the shadows, but when he saw her face he was shocked to the core. He had visited her once or twice at the hospital, but then she had been swathed in bandages, so it was only now that he saw the full extent of her injuries. Gathering all his courage, he looked straight at her without flinching and said, "I was the one pulled you out of the barn; saving them boys was the bravest thing I've ever seen."

"Well I wish like hell you'd left me in there!" she retorted, and he was shocked for a moment.

"You don't mean that," he said emphatically, "you might think you do now, but you've got a lot to live for."

"Oh yes," she said bitterly, "I've got such wonderful prospects. I could always get a job as a scarecrow. I'm so hideous that I'd scare anybody!"

"That's only on the surface, you'm still you underneath."

"Yes, but people only see the surface, don't they? Tell me then Jed," May challenged him, "what on earth have I got to live for?"

Jed sighed, thought a moment, and then shrugged and said lamely, "Well, the Squire's letting you stay on in this lovely cottage, and you'm surrounded by beautiful countryside…"

"But I can't go out to enjoy it looking like this, can I?" she cried, "and the cottage is my prison now!"

Jed continued "You can still read books, and there be a whole other world in books, and reading is something I can't do."

"You don't understand," May told him, "I'll never be able to have a husband and a family to love me, I'll never be able to teach and I'll never be able to travel or find a friend…"

"I'm your friend," he interjected firmly, "and so is the Squire, and he'll always look out for you, and so will I."

May was touched, for she could see he meant every word, but he had no concept of how lonely she was. It had been bad enough before the fire, but at least she'd had a future to look forward to, now there was nothing but empty days, stretching out to infinity.

When Jed left her he was deeply moved. He had faced up to her horrific injuries bravely, not letting her see how the sight of her had repulsed him, but now in the privacy of the woods, he broke down and wept bitter tears. He shook his fist at the sky and shouted angrily "God, why did you let May suffer like that?" It was so unfair that someone as lovely as her should have been so destroyed. She was the kindest person he knew, and she had never laughed at his inability to read, even when the other children at school had teased him and called him thick. He resolved that come what may he would do everything possible to make her life easier.

He had been sweet on May at school, but when she got engaged to James Bland and had rejected him he realised sadly that he could not compete with someone as smart and well educated as James, and so he had given up on her and had courted Nellie, the milkman's daughter. She had always tried to engage his interest when they were at school, but in those days he'd only had eyes for May, but now he realised that Nellie was great fun to be with, and they enjoyed teasing and winding each other up. She wasn't beautiful like May, being short and inclined to plumpness, but she had a lively personality and an easy smile, and she let him have his way with her after only the second date. When she fell pregnant he had felt obliged to marry her, but she suited him and they were comfortable together, and he had never regretted it.

Jed confided to his wife how much May's disfigurement had upset him, and urged her to go and visit with her and keep her company, but Nellie had shaken her head and told him, "I can't face her Jed, it would be too upsetting for me and especially for little Joanie, but you go as often as you want, I won't mind." With Nellie's blessing Jed became a frequent caller, and though they had an eighteen-month old baby and another on the way, he somehow always found time to do a few chores for May and her mother.

May was reluctant to be seen in public, and did not go out of the house for several weeks, but at Mrs Turner's urging she eventually agreed to accompany her to church. However, she immediately regretted her decision, for the horrified stares and embarrassed glances from people were upsetting enough, but then a young girl screamed and a couple of young children began to cry in terror at her appearance. After the service the vicar approached her nervously and said, "How are you getting on May? It's good to see you back with us, but I must request in future that you and your mother would kindly wait until the congregation are all seated before you come in and take a place at the back. Quite a few of my parishioners were rather upset, and I hope you understand that I can't afford to lose any of my flock."

Mrs Turner was up in arms and ready to do battle, but May said quietly, "It's alright Mother, I'll wear a veil in future." From then on she wore a heavy black veil to church, leaning on her mother's arm, for she could scarcely see through the thick material, but at least it stopped her having to witness the pitying and horrified looks from the congregation.

Chapter 8

One day May received a letter and was intrigued to see a Devon postmark. She knew no-one in the West Country, so was surprised to see that it was from James' mother. Mrs Bland had visited May at the hospital a couple of times and had wept to see her all swathed in bandages. She had cried "Oh if only Violet hadn't got pregnant, May would be married to James instead, and this would never have happened!"

Mrs Turner had thought along those lines herself, but she did not voice her opinion and merely said, "It's no good thinking about what might have been, what's done is done and we just have to live with the consequences."

Mrs Bland had told May that she would visit again and offered her support once she was released from hospital, but then out of the blue she had received a telegram informing her that her sister in Torquay had been partially paralysed by a stroke and needed looking after. She ran a small guest house, so as well as caring for her sister, Mrs Bland stayed to help in order to keep her business going, and she never returned to Lower Bulford.

She wrote to May asking how she was and invited her to stay while she recuperated, saying that the sea air would be an aid to her recovery, but May screwed the letter up angrily and threw it into the fire, telling her mother "I can't bloody well go anywhere looking like this, can I?"

"No," Mrs Turner agreed, "but it was kind of her to ask, and you should write her a note to thank her for the invitation." May duly wrote a brief letter of thanks and explained that she could not go out in public looking as she did, but then Mrs Bland wrote again and encouraged her not to give up on her dream of going to teacher's training college.

May snorted with disgust and said, "Listen to this rubbish Mum... and once your scars have faded you'll be amazed what a good covering of make-up will do for your confidence... the woman hasn't got a bloody clue, has she?"

"She hasn't any idea how badly you were scarred May," Mrs Turner said gently. "You were all covered in bandages when she visited you, so how could she possibly have known?"

May shrugged, and though she realised that Mrs Bland was being kind and had meant well, she didn't bother to reply to her letter, and she never heard from her again.

Old Mrs Turner died a couple of years later after a double dose of pneumonia, and then May felt even more isolated and lonely than before and decided to ask Jed if he would accompany her to church on Sunday. "I ain't no church-goer May," he had retorted, "and I don't need no jumped up parson in a frock telling me what to think. I finds God out in the woods where it's peaceful, and you'm welcome to come with me if you like."

She did go with him on a couple of occasions, but then she began to go on her own, taking pleasure in watching the rabbits early in the morning, and sometimes catching sight of a fox or a badger. Her favourite place was down by the stream on the edge of the Squire's land, and there she would spend many happy hours, trailing her fingers in the water and watching the water-boatmen and the colourful, darting dragonflies, and then she would be lulled into an almost meditative state by the gurgling water and the hum of insects. To get there she had to walk through an avenue of beech trees and the tall, straight trunks with the sunlight filtering through the arched branches always reminded her of the nave of a church.

One day, lured out by the glorious spring sunshine, she took a stroll through the woods, taking pleasure in the sounds of birdsong and the sound of the cuckoo heralding the approach of summer. The delicate scent of bluebells suffused the air and she picked a few to put in a vase in her kitchen and then, having wandered further than usual, she heard the sound of children's voices and edged nearer. Careful to keep hidden, she saw through a gap in the shrubbery the Squire's grandsons playing with some children from the village. She watched with pleasure as they played a game of tag but the youngest, Peter, suddenly laughed, pulled a hideous face and, tucking his left hand up his sleeve, asked, "Guess who I am?"

"May Turner!" crowed his brother.

Peter replied lustily "Yeah, and I'm coming to get you!" proceeding to run after the screaming children, delighting in their mock horror.

May flushed with anger and shame and she shrank back. She had felt an overpowering urge to grab him by the scruff of the neck and shout, "I look like this because I saved your miserable little lives, you ungrateful brats!" but of course she couldn't do it. Hot tears stung her eyes, and she blundered blindly back through the undergrowth, dropping the bluebells and unmindful of the stinging nettles and the branches that scratched her face and caught in her hair, just desperate to get back to the sanctuary of her cottage.

The incident had shaken her fragile confidence, and she never went near that part of the estate again, and if she did hear children's voices, would hide herself until they had passed by. She never mentioned this incident to Jed as she felt ashamed, not just for herself, but for the boys, and she knew that Jed would most probably go charging round to the manor and confront them, and it would be upsetting for the Squire to know how his grandsons had behaved.

Jed kindly did all May's weekly shopping at the little general store in the village, and occasionally he rode the six miles to Upper Bulford if there was something she needed that could not be bought locally, and then he would use Nellie's bicycle because it had a large basket strapped to the handlebars. He would always give her a hand with the heavy chores, chopping wood and digging the garden, spending as much time as he could spare, and she knew that she would never have been able to manage without his help.

One day she had begged him to cut her hair. When her mother was alive she had always washed and brushed May's hair and tidied it into a bun, but now she was finding it a struggle to cope with it single-handed, and it hung down in a straggly tangle.

"I ain't never cut no-one's hair before, May," Jed had replied diffidently, "I might make a right mess of it."

May had laughed and said, "It can't be a worse mess than it is now," and she had pressed the scissors into his unwilling hand.

Tentatively he began to hack away at May's locks, and he reflected sadly how lovely she still was when viewed from the right side and her awful disfigurement could not be seen. When he had reached the level of her earlobes she said, "That's enough Jed, I can manage it now," and she shook her head, delighted with the feeling if lightness and freedom her new hair cut gave her, even though it looked as if the rats had been chewing at it. Jed was no hairdresser, being more used to clipping hedges, but no-one else was going to see her, so what did it matter?

Chapter 9

After several years had passed May had more or less come to terms with her injuries, but she knew that her life could never be any different to what it was at that moment, though on warm, sunny days when she was able to sit in the garden breathing in the scent of honeysuckle, and drinking a glass of Jed's homemade elder flower wine, she was almost happy. She devoured books and had the run of Squire Bulford's extensive library, reading everything she could lay her hands on.

One day, when she had just finished re-reading *Jane Eyre* and was sitting pensively at the kitchen table, Jed called round with some fruit and vegetables from his garden. She thanked him and, as she busied herself in making tea, told him what she had just read. "Do you remember the story of Jane Eyre Jed?"

"Aye, we done that at school as I recall."

"That's right, and do you remember when Mr Rochester is burned and goes blind Jed, but then Jane comes back to him and she still loves him as much as ever?" Jed nodded and she sighed and said wistfully, "If only I could meet a blind man, someone who could love me for who I am and not how I look."

Jed shifted uncomfortably and said, "I don't know of any blind men, May, I'm sorry."

"I wish I'd let James have his way with me," she said bitterly. "I'll probably die and never know what it's like to love a man."

She began to weep, and Jed put his arms round her and patted her shoulder clumsily, saying, "There now May, don't go on so."

Eventually she stopped crying and asked "Do you remember you asked me to marry you once?" Jed nodded, but had a sinking feeling where this was leading, and May continued "And you kissed me, remember?"

"Aye, I'll never forget that," he smiled and she began hesitantly to ask, "I don't suppose, I mean, could you ever possibly…?"

Jed extricated himself gently and shook his head. "Now you know better'n to ask me that. I'm your good friend, but that's all, and anyway, I'm a happily married man."

"I'm sorry, Jed, I just get so damn lonely," replied May quickly, and then asked curiously, "What's it like, you know, making love? Is it really wonderful?"

Jed chuckled, "Aye, it can be, specially at first when you're crazy in love, but most of the time it's just like scratching an itch."

May burst out laughing and then, with the tension broken between them, they drank their tea and the talk turned to the safer topic of gardening.

Jed had taken to heart what May had said, and he thought sadly how beautiful she had been, and how he had always longed to kiss her. But things were different now, and though he still loved her, his stomach turned at the thought of touching her ruined face in that way. Realising that she needed something to love, he brought her a pair of black and white kittens that needed a good home, and May was enchanted by them. They didn't care what she looked like, and sat on her lap purring contentedly as she stroked them, and as she petted and played with them, May was as close to being happy as she had been for a very long time.

Time passed slowly for May, but eventually she grew accustomed to her solitary life and there were times when she felt at peace and contented with her lot. The winters were hard for her however, and she longed for springtime when she could get out into the grounds of Bulford Manor. One year there was an especially wet spring followed by a very hot summer, and the honeysuckle that grew over the house ran rampant, and started to grow into her bedroom window so that she could no longer close it properly.

The next time that Jed came by she asked him if he would trim it for her. "I'm rather afraid of losing my balance on that little balcony" she told him, "so would you be an angel and cut it back so that I can close my window. You don't mind, do you?"

"'Course I don't mind," replied Jed, "you knows I'm glad to give you a hand, but let's have a cold drink first as I'm right parched after the ride over here, and then I'll get cracking."

They sat outside in the shade of the house sipping glasses of cool, home-made lemonade and Jed noticed that May was wearing a floral button-through dress that he'd not seen before. "That's a pretty frock May. Is it new?"

"It's one of Violet's old ones," she smiled. "I've got thinner and it fits now. Do you like it?"

"Aye, it suits you," he said. "You should always wear blue." He drained his glass and fetched the secateurs from the saddle-bag of his bicycle. "Shall I go on up?" he asked.

She nodded. "You know the way."

She watched him step out onto the little balcony and begin hacking away at the honeysuckle. He was tanned a deep mahogany, and with his shirt open and sleeves rolled up she could see the hard muscles of his arms. He was handsome in a rough and ready kind of way, and she remembered the time when they were teenagers and he had kissed her. He had begged her to marry him then, but she had just become engaged to James and only had eyes for him, but she reflected on how different her life would have been if she had said yes to Jed. Doubtless she would have had a couple of children, and maybe even a job teaching at the local school, but it was no good thinking about what might have been. She sighed and watched Jed toss down the clippings, and he called down to her "Don't worry, I'll sweep it all up before I goes."

"I'm not worried," she smiled, "I'm just enjoying watching you work."

"Cheek!" he laughed. "Tis alright for some!"

The heat was making her feel languorous, and she tried to recall the feel of Jed's lips on hers all those years ago, and she had an intense longing to be held and made love to, and after a few moments she got up and went inside. As May entered her bedroom Jed was just finishing up and said, "Tis all cleared away now, so..." but the words died on his lips as he saw that she had unbuttoned her dress and was stark naked beneath. His eyes were glued to her full breasts and the dark triangle of hair between her legs, but he stammered "W...what are you d...doing May?"

73

"Make love to me Jed," she begged, "please, just this once so that I know what it feels like."

"No, 't wouldn't be right," he gasped, but she came towards him and put her hand on his crotch, and he grew hard in spite of his protestations.

He reached out and began to caress her breasts, and she moaned "Oh yes please Jed," and he deliberately didn't look at her ruined face but bent instead to suck her nipples, and her hand caressed the back of his neck.

May lay back on the bed and he unbuttoned his trousers and let them drop to the floor and she gasped, "Good Lord Jed, that's huge!" she had never properly seen a man erect before and was shocked at the size and protested, "That's never going to fit inside me!"

"'Course it will May," chuckled Jed. "I'll take it slow, don't worry." How badly he had wanted this moment all his teenage years, it had been all he dreamt about, but now it was May who longed for it and he didn't have the heart to disappoint her. He touched the secret place between her legs and she moaned softly as he slipped two fingers inside her, but she gave a little cry as his penis entered her.

He began to move, gently at first and then with more urgency, and then she was lost in pleasure, crying, "Oh yes Jed, please don't stop!"

Eventually he finished and rolled off her and quickly pulled up his trousers, but he could not look at her, nor could he help asking "Was it alright then?"

"Oh yes! Thank you Jed, it was lovely," sighed May ecstatically, "and I can die happy now."

"You knows we shouldn't really have done that," Jed said softly, "t'wasn't right."

"I don't care. I'm glad we did and I just needed to know what it was like to make love, and it was wonderful," May replied.

"I'd better go and tidy up the garden," said Jed feeling a little ashamed that he'd given in so easily, but she had completely taken him by surprise. If Nellie ever found out he'd be dead meat, so he would make certain that it never happened again.

Chapter 10

After their honeymoon, Doreen and Raymond moved into Honeysuckle Cottage, but they both knew it would not be easy with no electricity, and the old fashioned range that proved a devil to light. Help came in the form of Jed Fuller, who got the stove going and advised them to always keep it alight, but that was easier said than done, especially when both of them liked their bed in the morning. It took a good few attempts and a lot of swearing before Raymond got it relit, but it was essential for their hot water, tea and cooking facilities.

The cottage was in the village of Lower Bulford and, while it was very pretty, there was only one general store cum post office, a tea-room and the pub. For any major shopping and the launderette they had a twenty-minute drive to Upper Bulford which, though it sounded quite grand, was a rather ordinary town, with no distinguishing features, but it had a co-op and a couple of good butchers shops, and they often did their weekly shopping there.

Raymond had been forced to bow to imminent fatherhood by affixing a side-car onto his beloved Triumph motorcycle, for Doreen's belly had grown too large to comfortably ride pillion, and anyway they would need it for when the baby came. He had found a job as a trainee mechanic in Upper Bulford, and while he was at work Doreen painted the bedrooms and attempted to sew a few baby clothes. She often wondered whereabouts her aunt had died, and hoped it had not been in their bed, but there was nothing to give her a clue, as Jed had thoroughly scrubbed away the blood from the flagstones in front of the range and thrown away the blood-stained quilt. Sometimes, as she went about her chores, she felt as if she was being watched, but she told herself she was being fanciful, but all the same it was unsettling.

Doreen didn't really mind the housework, although she constantly had to heat up enough water on the range, but she did find cooking was a real chore, and struggled to provide them with a decent evening meal. She was still not used to the range, and most nights Raymond would be obliged to sit down to burnt offerings.

A couple of weeks before the baby was due to arrive her mother turned up unannounced with Uncle Harry. She came bearing gifts, however, a knitted layette from her friend Rita, a baby bath that Doreen had not even thought about getting, and two sets of cot blankets and sheets. Harry gave her a carrycot on wheels that could double as a pram, but once detached it would do as the baby's bed until they could afford a proper cot.

Violet was very concerned about her daughter being on her own in the cottage all day and asked her, "What on earth are you going to do if the baby comes while Raymond's at work?"

"I don't know Mum," Doreen replied quietly, "I don't really want to think about it."

"Well, you have to think about it," her mother chided her. "You're very isolated here without a telephone, and there are no neighbours nearby to help you. I think you should pack your things and stay with me until the baby's born, what do you think Harry?"

"I agree with your mother Doreen. You can't possibly be alone here when your baby arrives."

Doreen knew her mother was right, and she had to admit that she'd been worried too, but she knew that Raymond would not be too happy about it. When Raymond arrived home tired from work supper was not ready, and he was not best pleased to see Violet and Harry, and said stiffly, "Mrs Bland, Mr Marvel, this is a surprise."

"They brought some things for the baby, Ray," said Doreen quickly. "Isn't that kind?"

"Yeah, thanks," he said grudgingly, and looked pointedly at the stove.

"Sorry Raymond, I haven't had time to do any tea yet…" Doreen apologised.

Harry interjected "Why don't I treat us all to a meal at that nice pub in the village?"

Raymond perked up at the thought of a large juicy steak and chips, and swiftly changed out of his overalls and had a quick wash at the kitchen sink. Over dinner Violet brought up the subject of Doreen returning home with her for the birth, but Raymond was selfishly thinking only about himself. "What am I gonna do all on my tod?" he asked peevishly.

"You'll manage, you can eat at the chippie near your work," replied Doreen tartly, "and it would only be for a couple of weeks." He said nothing, but stared moodily at his plate, and Doreen continued, "I'm scared to be on my own Ray, what happens if the baby comes while you're at work?"

"I hadn't thought really," he said, and then softening added, "I suppose it makes sense, at least then I won't have to worry about you."

Doreen gave birth to a daughter three weeks later, and named her Daisy-May, and Raymond arrived on the following Sunday to fetch them home in the side-car. He had been hoping for a boy, someone he could play football with and who would share his love of all things mechanical, but when he caught sight of his little daughter he was instantly smitten. She was so beautiful, and every time she looked at him with her big blue eyes, his heart melted.

When they got home and Doreen walked into the kitchen, she was shocked at the state of the place. Raymond had not lifted a finger while she'd been away, and virtually every cup and plate was dirty, piled into the sink and waiting for her to wash them. The range was lit, just, but there was ash and dirt all over the floor, and when she went upstairs there were oily stains on the sheets where he had thrown his filthy overalls. When she chastised him he said, "Oh stop nagging Doreen, it's not man's work, is it? I'm going for a drink!"

Doreen heated up the kettle, fed and changed the baby and then laid her down to sleep in her carrycot before tackling the mountains of dirty dishes. Luckily Daisy-May was not a fretful baby and went straight off to sleep, so she was able to finish it all before Raymond returned from the pub, and she was just changing the sheets on their bed when he arrived home. He was in a good mood after wetting the baby's head, but that soon changed when Doreen thrust the filthy sheets at him and said, "You'll have to take these to the launderette tomorrow."

"I haven't got time to do that," he said indignantly.

She retorted, "Well, if you think I'm going to scrub them in that tin bath out there, you can jolly well think again!"

They made it up later on in bed that night and Raymond, snuggling up to her said, "I'm really glad you're back, babe, I didn't like it here on my own, the place gives me the creeps."

Neither of them was finding married life easy, and for Doreen it was a never ending round of drudgery. She hadn't realised just how many nappies little Daisy-May would get through in a day, and as she had to boil the water each time to hand wash them, she wondered how her aunt had coped, literally single-handed.

Actually, May had coped pretty well. She had rubbed the clothes clean on the washboard and wrung them out through the mangle, but the sheets were rather too much for her to cope with once her mother was no longer there to help. Thankfully, Jed Fuller offered to take them up to the Manor to be boiled in their big copper, and he brought them back cleaned, starched and pressed. There wasn't much that May couldn't do, but Jed helped her with those chores that she found too much of a struggle.

Violet had been relieved when Doreen had moved out, as relations between them had been tense ever since they had learned of May's death, but now she missed her daughter's presence around the house, even if it was to let off steam after a particularly frustrating day at work. It was strange to think that she and Raymond were now living in her old childhood home and that she was not entitled to have anything from her past. It had hurt her when May had left everything to Doreen, but she was not really surprised, and truth be told she would do the same all over again, but she wished heartily that her daughter had not found out the truth about the feud between herself and May.

The winter months were hard and lonely for Doreen, who knew no-one in the village, and the cottage, apart from the kitchen, was cold and damp. She really missed her friends, and when little Daisy-May got sick with a feverish cold, Doreen decided she'd had enough, and bursting into tears told her husband "It's no good Raymond, we can't stay here. I can't cope any more."

She was tempted to write to her mother and ask if they could move in with her, but Raymond was not happy about that and put his foot down. "No Doreen, we're not going crawling to your mother, we'll go and see mine and see if she can put us up."

They decided to visit Mrs Smith the following day and were pleasantly surprised when she made the suggestion that they live with her. She offered them Raymond's brother's room, as he had moved out a couple of weeks before and found a job in London, and she confessed that she was feeling rather lonely in the house on her own.

"It would be lovely to have some company," she had told them "and I'd be handy for baby-sitting, wouldn't I?"

That made up their minds, and without further ado they agreed to move in as soon as they could, and although it would be a little cramped with the baby sleeping in their room, at least it was warm and dry, and Doreen would have help with the care of little Daisy. After a lot of heart searching, they decided to put Honeysuckle Cottage on the market.

ROSA

Chapter 11

Rosa Montford was at the end of her tether. She had been trying to work on her painting, but ever since the young people had moved in upstairs she'd had to put up with constant noise. They had a seemingly never ending stream of visitors, with parties virtually every other night, and the continuous blaring of their pop music made her feel constantly tired and tetchy.

From a large comfortable home in Chelsea she had been forced to move to a pokey one-bedroom flat in Westbourne Grove, because once their son Rupert had left home for medical college, her husband had asked her for a divorce. It had come as a huge shock, for although they had led fairly separate lives, she'd had no idea that her husband of twenty years was having an affair with his secretary. Leo had confessed that it had been going on for some time, and now his lover was pregnant. There was more bad news, and she thought how strange it was that bad luck never came singly. Her husband had invested rather unwisely on the stock market, and lost virtually all their savings, so therefore they would be forced to sell their beloved house in Chelsea as quickly as possible.

Rosa was almost more upset at losing the home she had lavished her attention on than losing her husband. Their home had been a lovely Georgian building in a quiet, elegant square, and it had high ceilings and large windows that let in plenty of light, and she had filled it with flowers and period pieces of furniture. Regretfully, most of it had to be sold along with the house, but she managed to keep one or two of the smaller pieces; a mahogany writing table and a pair of chairs upholstered with needlework seats that her mother had stitched, and Leo had kept a few heirlooms from his parent's home, and the rest had been sent to auction.

The one-bedroom flat she had bought was only partially furnished, with a double bed and built-in wardrobe taking up all the space in the cramped bedroom, and a hideous sofa that she covered up with a bedspread in the slightly larger living-room. She had intended to replace this just as soon as she could afford to, and was prepared to wait for the January sales so that she would get a good deal.

There was also a stained dining-table with flaps that could be raised to make it longer, and on this she did her paintings, but with the furniture she had brought with her there was not enough room to swing a cat, and the place was stuffy because she usually kept the window closed. When the window was open, the room was suffused with the smell of curry from the Indian restaurant downstairs, and the road was so noisy it made her head ache.

When their Chelsea house was sold, Leo had given her a choice; she could have half the price of whatever the house fetched and take care of their son Rupert's needs, or he would give her a third and invest the remainder for their son, giving him a small private income. After careful consideration, Rosa opted for the second choice, for she thought it was high time that

Rupert took charge of his own finances, as her husband had not proved himself to be a very safe investor.

Rupert was her much loved son but, as an only child, he had been rather indulged and expected things to go on the way they had. She and Leo had wanted to give him a brother or sister, and had tried hard to make it a reality, but she had suffered two miscarriages before he was born, and afterwards it just hadn't happened, even though she had endured all sorts of tests.

She had invested the money that was left after buying the flat and, to eke out the tiny allowance, she worked three days a week selling soft furnishings in Whiteleys' department store, and occasionally sold some of her work along the railings on the Bayswater road on a Sunday. She now jumped up to close the window in order to block out the siren of an approaching fire-engine when she knocked a bottle of Indian ink all over the painting she had been painstakingly working on. "Damn and blast!" she swore. It was spoiled now, and she would have to begin her work all over again.

The phone rang just as she was mopping up the ink, and she must have sounded rather curt, as her friend Joy asked, "Is it a bad time? I can call back later."

"No, sorry, it's only that I've just ruined a piece of work," replied Rosa.

Joy commiserated with her and said, "Sorry to hear that, but the reason I phoned was to see if you fancied a week's painting holiday in the country?"

"Oh that sounds lovely, when is it?"

"Next Sunday. I know it's short notice, but it's at a really nice place called Bulford Manor."

"I'd love to go," sighed Rosa wistfully, "but it does rather depend on the cost."

"Well, I suppose it is a bit on the pricey side," said Joy ruefully, "but it does include breakfast and dinner, and it's in such a beautiful spot. Anyway, you deserve a bit of a break. When was the last time you had a holiday?" Rosa let herself be persuaded, even though it meant digging deep into her savings, but a peaceful week in the country was just what she craved.

She was finding it rather hard to adjust to living in the busy, cosmopolitan Queensway area where there was a vibrant nightlife, and even though it was convenient to have all the shops that stayed open late and a great choice of restaurants at hand, she would have traded them all for the peace and quiet of the little square in Chelsea that she had lived in all her adult life.

She had first met her friend Joy at art classes after her marriage broke up, and though she had always been artistic, it had all been channelled into the decorating of the Chelsea house. However, now that she needed to earn her own living, Rosa had wanted to learn to paint properly, and though she showed great talent, it was proving very difficult to make any money from it.

They had picked a good time to go to Bulford Manor, for the weather was warm and sunny and was expected to stay that way for the entire week. There were twenty-four people on the sketching holiday, mostly elderly, retired people, but there was one young man in his thirties who seemed to take a shine to Rosa.

She was a small, slim woman in her early fifties, but looked at least ten years younger. She had a heart shaped face framed by glossy dark hair, although peppered with a few grey ones, and she wore it in a shoulder length bob and cut with a fringe that accentuated her large dark eyes. Joy told her a little enviously that she always managed to look elegant, even in jeans, and teased her that she had an admirer, but Rosa blushed and said,

"Don't be silly, he's young enough to be my son," but nonetheless it did wonders for her self confidence.

On one of the days spent painting in the village Rosa decided to wander off by herself. Most of the others had congregated around the church or the pub to paint, but she wanted somewhere different, and also wanted to escape the unwanted attentions of the young man. He was nice looking and rather sweet, but very persistent, and she was just not interested in a romantic liaison.

Eventually she came to a narrow lane and, as she turned the corner, was enchanted to find a small tumbledown cottage with gothic arched windows and a mass of sweet scented honeysuckle spilling over the porch. A faded sign on the gate said Honeysuckle Cottage, and she quickly set up her stool and easel and began to paint. It was the best thing she'd done for ages, and when she had placed the final brushstroke, she decided to explore further.

The door was locked, but peering through the grimy window she could make out a range in the large, old-fashioned kitchen and a staircase leading to the first floor. Following a path down the side of the house, she pushed her way through overgrown shrubs and came upon a large, walled, sunny garden. The grass was almost waist high, but among the weeds she could see some pink climbing roses, some foxgloves, a cluster of delphiniums and a host of other perennials fighting for space, and the air was delightfully scented with the roses and honeysuckle. She thought how sad it was that such a lovely garden had been so neglected, and she would have loved to bring it back to some sort of order.

As she turned around towards the house she gasped in surprise at the huge gothic window that was completely out of scale with the tiny cottage, and above it another large arched window with a small wrought iron balcony that was smothered in honeysuckle. Rosa thought how wonderful it would be to wake to the scent of that instead of curry and traffic fumes wafting into her flat and, as she made her way back to the gate, she almost tripped over an estate agents' 'For Sale' sign that had fallen over and was half-buried in the undergrowth. It was very faded, but she could just about make out the letters so, taking out her sketch pad, she noted their name and number, and resolved to give them a call later.

She had arranged to meet up with Joy at four in the village tea-rooms cum art gallery, and as she glanced at her watch, saw that it was almost four o'clock already. Her friend had thoughtfully ordered tea and scones as Rosa breathlessly entered and sat herself down.

"I've just seen my dream house, look..." she said excitedly and took out her sketch pad to show Joy, "... and I'm going to phone the estate agents tomorrow and arrange a viewing."

Joy was quite taken by surprise and said, "What, seriously, you're thinking of buying a cottage?"

"Yes," Rosa smiled, "it's so peaceful here, and I could paint to my heart's content and no-one would bother me."

"But how on earth are you going to live?"

"I don't know yet," mused Rosa, "it depends on the price of the cottage. Will you come and view it with me?"

"Just try and stop me!" laughed Joy.

"Excuse me..." the proprietor of the tea-rooms hovered behind their table, "...may I just have a look at your watercolour?"

Rosa was surprised, for she hadn't realised that anyone else had seen her painting, but she handed it over willingly.

"Oh this is excellent work," the woman exclaimed, and then asked "I wonder would you consider putting this for sale here in the gallery? Only it's just the sort of thing that the tourists would love."

"Well, yes, that would be marvellous," Rosa replied, amazed that the woman had been so enthusiastic about her work, and thought perhaps it was a good omen.

When she phoned the estate agents in the morning to make an appointment to view the cottage, the young man who answered the phone had never heard of it and said, "Just a moment please..."

She heard him asking someone in the background, and a moment later a woman took the receiver and said, "Yes, do you mean Honeysuckle Cottage in Lower Bulford?" When Rosa affirmed that it was the right house the agent said, "It's been on our books for quite a number of years and it needs to be completely modernised, and you do realise there's no electricity?" Rosa hadn't known, but it didn't put her off, and she made an appointment to see it the following day.

When they arrived at the cottage, the agent was already waiting for them, and she unlocked the stout oak door and pushed it open with a loud creaking of hinges. "Needs a little oil," she said apologetically and showed them into the kitchen. It was large, but quite dark, for the two arched windows either side of the door were grimy with dirt and partially obscured by honeysuckle. Rosa loved the big old range, the Belfast sink, the stone flagged floor and the pine dresser, and in fact it was just the sort of kitchen she had always dreamt about.

The agent then threw open the door into the other room and Rosa gave a little gasp of delight. The room was flooded with light from the big gothic window, a complete contrast to the gloom of the kitchen, and she saw there were French-doors that opened out into the garden.

"Oh, it's perfect!" she cried, "I could really paint here, there's so much light." She also loved the arched bookcases either side of the mantelpiece, and asked the agent if the fire-place was usable.

"Yes," she replied, "but I think you'll need to get the chimney swept first."

Rosa stood admiring the layout of the garden, daydreaming about what she would do with it, but the estate agent broke into her thoughts and asked "Would you like to see upstairs now?" Rosa nodded, although she would have liked to spend all day in this room, but the agent was anxious to be off. There were two equal-sized rooms upstairs, and the back bedroom with the big window overlooking the garden still had its original Victorian furniture in it, and Rosa asked if it was to be included with the house. "Yes, the house would come with all its contents," the agent assured her, "as the vendors live a long way from here and don't want to have the bother of clearing it all out."

"That's good," said Rosa, and ran her hands lovingly over the wrought iron bedstead. She could do so much with this room, and imagined herself sitting out on the little balcony in the summer painting the flowers in the garden. The other bedroom at the front had two arched dormer windows, but rather utilitarian furniture that she would probably get rid of.

"Where's the bathroom?" asked Joy.

The agent apologised, saying "There's no bathroom I'm afraid, but there's an outside lavatory and a wash-house, come, I'll show you."

They dutifully followed her downstairs and she showed them the wash-house which contained a tin bath and an iron mangle, and Rosa wondered how the previous occupants had managed.

"It is on the main water supply, isn't it?" asked Joy.

The woman nodded, "Yes, but there's no hot water, everything has to be heated up on the range."

Rosa had a good look at the roof, and it appeared to be alright, so now she asked the agent the price of the cottage. "Well," the woman said, "it was on the market for £5,000, but it's been on our books for so long that the owner would probably be glad of any offer you'd care to make."

"How about £3,500 for a quick sale?" said Rosa quickly, hoping they would agree. It was all she had in her investment account, but if she sold her flat in Westbourne Grove she could pay for the modernisation of Honeysuckle Cottage and still have enough left over to live on.

"I'll phone my clients and give them your offer, but there is just one thing..." she laughed nervously, "...it's supposed to have a ghost. I just thought I'd better tell you."

Rosa smiled, "That doesn't worry me. You can reach me at Bulford Manor till the end of the week."

Things suddenly began to look up for Rosa. Her offer was accepted, and then her painting sold, the gallery owner giving her the princely sum of £25 and asking if she had any more pictures to give her. She was keen to get back to London and put her flat up for sale, as she wanted to have the bulk of the work done at the cottage before the winter set in. Joy thought she was mad to move to such an isolated and run-down cottage, but Rosa had never been more sure of anything. It was going to be heaven.

Chapter 12

Rosa got the keys the last week in July, and her son Rupert took a few days off from his hospital duties to help move her stuff down to the cottage. He hadn't seen it before, so he was quite shocked at its run-down state.

"We can't possibly stay here Mother," he told her firmly, "I'll book us into the pub for bed and breakfast, and then we'll have to find someone to tackle the work."

Rosa's flat in London was under offer, but until the sale came through she would have no money to pay the builders, so she paid a visit to the bank in Upper Bulford to ask the manager to give her a bridging loan. As soon as it came through they hired builders, an electrician and a plumber, for she had decided to split the front bedroom to make a bathroom and a single bedroom, which would be quite spacious enough if Rupert or Joy came to stay. She decided to buy a new mattress for the wrought iron bed, and then somehow charmed the man into taking away the old one, and then she bought paint and cleaning materials ready to tackle the decorating once the electrician had finished.

In the pub that evening Rosa was approached by an elderly man. He was lean and wiry and nut brown, with sinewy arms on which the veins stood out like blue cords, and he sported a pair of mutton-chop whiskers the like of which Rosa had only ever seen in books.

"Are you'm the lady that's bought Honeysuckle Cottage?" he asked her, and when Rosa said yes, he introduced himself.

"My name's Jed Fuller. I used to do a bit of work for the lady that lived there years ago, and I was wondering if you needed any help with the garden?"

"Oh yes please," said Rosa gratefully, "that would be wonderful, but I'm afraid I won't be able to afford to hire you till I sell my flat in London."

"Don't you worry 'bout that, you can pay me later. I'll come round tomorrow afternoon, if that's alright, and see what needs doing."

Jed arrived just after lunch looking like the grim reaper, carrying an enormous scythe and with his corduroy trousers tied up with garden twine, and said, "I thought I'd make a start on the grass; then we can see better what needs to be done." Rosa watched him work for a while, then got out her sketch pad and did a few drawings of him. He stopped to mop his brow with a red spotted handkerchief, saw her sketching, and asked, "You'm an artist then?"

"Yes," replied Rosa, "it's the reason why I bought the cottage, I wanted somewhere peaceful where I could paint."

"Well, you picked a right lovely spot, that's for sure."

"I'm sorry I can't offer you a cold drink," Rosa said ruefully, "but I'm afraid my fridge hasn't been delivered yet."

"Ah, tap-water'll do for me," said Jed, and once he had refreshed himself, he got back into the rhythm of scything.

"I don't suppose you know of a chimney sweep?" asked Rosa when he had done. "I'd really like to get the fireplace and the range going, and then perhaps you'd be kind enough to show me how to get it working."

"Aye, I does, and I'll get a man out to you next week. You'll be needing some logs I s'pose?"

"There's a few in the wood shed," said Rosa, "but I don't know how long they'll last me."

"Don't you worry," Jed reassured her, "leave it to me. I'll get you all you need."

Jed was turning out to be a real treasure. He came again the following day to trim back some of the honeysuckle and replace a couple of loose slates that he'd spotted. Once the grass was cut Rosa could see the edges of the herbaceous border, and had already begun the enormous task of weeding it. Jed gave her a hand and asked "Will you be growing your own vegetables?"

"I don't know," she replied, "I hadn't really given it much thought."

"Only if you are, it ain't too late to plant a few cabbages."

"I don't really know much about growing vegetables," confessed Rosa. "I only had a little courtyard garden in London, and there was only just room enough for a few pots of herbs."

"Well, if you likes," suggested Jed, "I could come regular, maybe once or twice a week and do over your garden for you, and I don't charge a lot."

"Oh that would be wonderful," cried Rosa happily, because she knew very little about managing a garden, and with Jed working for her it meant that she would have more time to paint.

Once the builders had finished, Rosa started to decorate the rooms, beginning with her bedroom. She had chosen to paint everything white for, until she had lived in a place for a while, she didn't know how she wanted it to look, and white was clean and fresh and let in the light.

When the bedroom was finished she moved in, delighting in the large wrought iron bed and the huge window that overlooked the garden. She unpacked an antique patchwork quilt that she had picked up for a song in the Portobello road, and it looked perfect on the bed. Then she hung a pretty gilt-framed mirror over the chest of drawers, and once she had arranged her perfume bottles and laid out her brush and comb, it already felt more homely.

Jed came round and showed her how to light the range saying, "That'll be good for all your hot water now, and all your cooking too, but mind you don't let it go out."

The plumber had fitted a hot water tank that connected to the range, so now she would be able to take a bath in her new bathroom any time she wanted. There had only been room for a shower at her Westbourne Grove flat, so she was really looking forward to the luxury of a nice leisurely soak in her new home. It took a few days to sort out all her stuff, but once her bits of furniture were in place, and her pictures hung, it began to really feel like home.

Yes, thought Rosa, *I'm going to be very happy here.*

Jed Fuller was happy too, as he had been sad to see May's old home going to rack and ruin, and now it was being brought back to life, and made much more comfortable. He had found life a bit of a struggle and money was tight after the Squire had died and the manor house had been closed up. It meant he had to try and find work wherever he could, and he'd sold logs that he cut from the estate, did a little poaching to supply his neighbours with game, and generally turned his hand to any odd jobs going.

Everyone had been wondering what would become of the manor, and those that had been employed there found themselves in dire straits without a job. There had been rumours that a property developer was buying the land and was going to demolish the manor house and build a housing estate, and Jed thought it would be criminal to pull down such a fine old house, but eventually, to everyone's relief, the manor had been sold, with the new owners turning it into a country house hotel, and then he had managed to get a permanent job as a gardener.

Now Jed came twice a week to do the garden, and Rosa could see it gradually coming back to the glory it had once been. She set up her easel at the French windows and began to paint, but once or twice she felt a presence, as if someone was looking over her shoulder. It didn't worry her too much, as she felt whoever it was didn't mean her any harm. When she had half a dozen watercolours of the cottage and its garden, she took them down to the little gallery in the village.

The owner of the gallery, Lizzie Appleby, was enchanted by her work, and to her delight had sold them all within a fortnight and begged her for more. It seemed as if Rosa's work was charmed, for every painting she did of the cottage sold almost straight away and, strangely enough, she didn't get bored with painting it.

When demand exceeded what she could supply, Lizzie had a bright idea. "Look, why don't you get some of your paintings printed up as greeting cards? I know I could sell plenty, and there are couple of shops in Upper

Bulford who I'm sure would be really glad to take them." Rosa thought it was a very good idea and, as the money from the sale of her flat had at last come through, was able to fund the printing.

She picked out two designs, one of them the front view of the cottage with the honeysuckle spilling over the porch, and the other one of the rear, painted from the far end of her garden, with the delphiniums and roses framing the large gothic window. It seemed as if every tourist that entered the tea-shop bought at least a card if they couldn't afford a painting, and some of them bought two. For the first time in her life Rosa was earning her own living by doing something she loved, and she felt she had the cottage to thank.

One day, when Jed had finished in the garden, Rosa made some tea and set out a freshly baked sponge cake, cutting him a large slice, and then asked him about who had lived in the cottage before her.

"Ah, that was May Turner," Jed told her, adding sadly "she was my good friend but she died tragically young,"

"Why, what happened to her?" Rosa asked curiously.

"She died of pneumonia I reckon," Jed explained, "and I found her laid down dead by that very chair by the fire."

May had been soaked in a heavy shower one day while walking out in the woods, and as a result had caught a bad cold which had gone on to her chest. Jed had called round to find her shivering and wheezing in the fireside chair, and had offered to help her up to bed, but she had declined, saying "No, I'm much warmer down here, and I can breathe better sitting up." He had stoked up the fire, fetched her quilt from the bedroom and made her a hot drink before taking his leave.

"I reckon I ought to get the doctor out to see you," he had said, but May had shaken her head and insisted that he wait to see how she was in the morning.

"Well, she were gone," said Jed sadly, "and I blames meself for not calling the doctor, 'cause her poor damaged lungs just couldn't cope."

"How sad," Rosa shivered, and asked "how did she damage her lungs, was it in the war?"

"No, t'was in a fire, and she was a true heroine," Jed told her and then took out his tobacco tin and began to make himself a roll-up, but Rosa offered him one of her filter tips and he said, "I don't mind if I do," and tucked the roll-up behind his ear to have later. He didn't think much of the cigarettes that Rosa smoked, as he reckoned they hardly had any taste, but he wasn't going to look a gift-horse in the mouth.

Rosa was curious to hear more about May's heroic deeds and asked Jed to carry on with his tale, but he looked pointedly at his empty cup and said slyly, "'Tis thirsty work, all this storytelling," and when she had poured him a fresh cup he proceeded to tell Rosa all about how May had rescued the Squire's grandsons.

"'Course, in the end it all turned out tragic for the Squire and all," said Jed reflectively.

"In what way?" asked Rosa, fascinated by his story, and poured him yet another cup of tea.

"I reckon he was cursed," Jed told her, "as both his sons was killed in the war and then he was left to bring up the grandchildren on his own. The mother of them boys had died a couple of years previous giving birth to her third child, and that poor mite was still-born, and then a couple of months after his sons were killed, his wife passed away. She weren't never very strong, and I reckon the grief finished her off."

"Poor man," said Rosa sympathetically, "it must have been a terrible time for him."

"Aye, it was. He was eternally grateful to May for saving his grandsons, and he done everything he could to make her life easier. Shame it was all for nothing though."

"What do you mean, all for nothing?" asked Rosa curiously and Jed sighed and continued with his story, but not before Rosa had cut him another slice of cake.

"When they grew up, them boys were a bit wild like, he'd spoiled 'em, let 'em have their own way too much. The oldest one had a car, a sports car t'was, and they'd go tearing round the countryside like lunatics. Rumour has it the night they died they'd been racing another local lad along Half Mile Lane, there's a humpty back bridge there..."

"Oh yes," interrupted Rosa, "I know exactly where you mean."

"Well, as you knows, there's only room for one car to pass, and the Squire's grandsons got there first, went over the bridge smack into a Land Rover coming the other way! Well, they had no chance, killed outright, and the youngest, Peter, had his head ripped off, it was terrible."

It had been Jed who had broken the news to May, and she had been devastated. "Oh no, Jed," she had cried, "poor Squire Bulford! Whatever will he do without those boys?"

"I don't rightly know," said Jed sadly, "he doted on 'em, and I don't reckon he'll want to go on." When Jed left she had wept, not just for the Squire, but for the terrible waste of the two young lives, and also for herself, because now it seemed as if her sacrifice had all been in vain.

She could not face going to the funeral and seeing the pitying glances and the subtle drawing back of people as she approached, but instead she lit two candles in her room and said a quiet prayer for the souls of the two young men. The following day she paid a visit to Squire Bulford but was really shocked by his appearance, for he seemed to have aged ten years in the last few weeks. His frame, already gaunt, was almost skeletal, and his sunken eyes looked dully out of dark, shadowed sockets. His hand trembled slightly as he offered it to her, but his voice was still strong as he thanked her for coming to see him.

"This is the worst business May, the cruellest trick of fate…" he was fighting the trembling of his lip, and May turned away to allow him to compose himself.

There were no words of comfort she could offer, so she just said, "I'll be there if you need me, you don't have to be alone."

A few days later she was not surprised to hear from Jed that the Squire had suffered a stroke. She then became a frequent visitor, bringing him homemade soups and reading to him in the dark winter evenings, but two weeks before Christmas he quietly slipped away. Rosa was horrified at the story and said, "Oh no, how awful, poor Squire Bulford. So he ended up losing everyone?"

"Aye, he did, and he weren't never the same after that," said Jed, adding, "but he left May the cottage and the grounds, and an allowance till the end of her days. She used to visit him sometimes, after his stroke, and read to him like. He had a fine library, and she loved books."

"What happened to the library after he'd gone?"

"I don't rightly know. I helped May to take a few of her favourites, but I reckon the rest must have been sold." He had managed to sweet talk the housekeeper into letting May have some of the books, and he also found an old wind-up gramophone and some records of dance music and loaded them into a wheelbarrow and took them down to the cottage. May had been thrilled by the gift of the gramophone, as without electricity she was unable to have wireless, but now she could once again listen to music.

May was even more isolated after the passing of the Squire, and she devoured books as her only means of escape from her lonely existence, but a year or two passed and her eyesight was not what it was. She desperately needed glasses, but could not bring herself to go to the doctor. Jed urged her to go, but she stubbornly refused, so when Nellie won a transistor radio as first prize in a raffle Jed persuaded his wife that it would be a great kindness to give it to May, as they already had an electronic wireless. May was overwhelmed with gratitude, as now she could hear plays, and music, and keep up with the latest news, and it made her feel connected to the world once again.

Eventually the batteries ran out, and Jed found her weeping at the kitchen table. "I don't know what I've done, but the radio's broken," she wailed.

Jed chuckled "It's only the batteries that's dead. I'll bring you some new ones tomorrow." He was as good as his word, and then May was content once more.

Jed had confided to Rosa how much he cared for May, and told her "I reckon May were very lonely in this cottage, and after the Squire died she only had me to talk to, and I ain't much company."

"Well, I've really enjoyed talking to you," said Rosa emphatically.

"And I've enjoyed sampling your cake," Jed said archly. "May always used to bake biscuits or a cake when I went round; she knew my missus wasn't much of a cook."

"In that case, I'll be sure to do some baking when you come next week," said Rosa with a smile, for it had been a long time since her culinary skills had been appreciated.

The air had a decidedly autumnal feel the following week, and Rosa did most of her painting indoors. The garden was coming on nicely and, as she began to paint a clump of Michaelmas daisies lit by the evening sun, she felt a presence behind her and a light touch on her shoulder. Turning quickly, she felt the hairs on the back of her neck prickle, for there was no-one there.

"Who's there? That you May?" she asked tentatively, "And if it is, please give me a sign."

Almost immediately one of her paint brushes rolled to the edge of her little painting table and fell to the floor. Rosa gasped, and said softly, "Hello May, I hope you approve of what I've done to your cottage." She felt the lightest touch brush her hair, and then the presence had gone.

She told Jed Fuller about it when he arrived the next day, and he said matter-of-factly, "Oh t'was May sure enough, but don't you worry 'bout her, she don't mean you no harm."

"I'm not worried," Rosa assured him, "she wasn't scary in the slightest."

"I know it sounds daft, but after she died I used to come up here sometimes and talk to her. I'd tell her all me troubles, and what was a doing in the garden, and I always felt she was there listening. It made me feel better anyway."

"Well I do hope she's not upset that I've taken over her cottage."

"Listen, if May was here now, she'd be right pleased that you've made it into a nice home again. She loved this place, and it must have made her sad to see it all neglected," Jed assured her.

"I never thought of that," said Rosa, "and you know it's strange, but it seems that since I moved here all my paintings are really selling well."

"There you are then, she's looking out for you," Jed chuckled, and helped himself to another slice of Rosa's delicious fruit cake.

Chapter 13

Rosa had settled well into village life and soon became firm friends with Lizzie Appleby from the art gallery. Lizzie had a beautiful contralto voice and sang in the church choir and also belonged to the local amateur dramatics society, and frequently enlisted Rosa to help out with painting the scenery and making the costumes. Although she didn't have the nerve to appear onstage herself, Rosa would sometimes help out as prompter, and she always made sure to attend first nights in the village hall, and then she would offer her help behind the scenes in getting the actors made-up and ready before the curtain went up.

Sometimes one of her London friends would come to stay for the weekend, but though she enjoyed their company, she found she didn't really miss the city at all. Her son Rupert visited occasionally but, as his life as a junior doctor was rather hectic, the visits were few and far between. The last time he had stayed he had told her that Leo and his new wife were expecting a second baby.

"I've always wanted a brother or sister," he said mournfully, and Rosa found herself apologising.

"I'm so sorry, dear, your father and I tried everything to have another baby, but it just wasn't to be."

The news that her ex-husband was going to be a father again had upset Rosa more than she had expected, but she didn't let Rupert see it. Privately she thought it was high time that he got married and had babies of his own, but she was far too tactful to broach the subject. However, she did ask him if there was anyone special in his life, and he replied "No Mother, I'm having far too much fun to think about settling down." She supposed he just hadn't met the right girl, but Rupert's idea of fun revolved around the roulette wheel or a pack of cards.

He had always enjoyed a bet, even at school he would get involved in card games during break time, often losing his dinner money and having to go without lunch. His friends gave him the nickname Joker, and when his mother asked why, he replied that it was because he was always telling them jokes. He did not wait around to elaborate, so she never realised that he'd been named that because he had once been caught hiding a joker up his sleeve when they played the game of twenty-one in order to win the pot.

Apart from medicine he was only really interested in gambling, but it was gradually beginning to take over his life. Even though he wasn't badly paid as a junior doctor, and had a small private income from the sale of the parental home, he always seemed to be short of money.

Rupert had recently tried to borrow some money from his father, but Leo had said a firm no, for with the imminent arrival of the new baby, there was just no money to spare. In desperation he paid Rosa a surprise visit and asked "Mother, I'm afraid I'm in a bit of a fix. I don't suppose you couldn't lend me a couple of grand, could you?"

"Darling," she had replied in astonishment, "it's wonderful to see you, but how come you need all that money?"

"I lost at poker if you must know," Rupert grudgingly admitted, and added, "and if I don't pay up in the next few days I could end up in casualty with a few broken bones."

"Oh Rupert," she said, horrified, "you shouldn't get involved with people like that. I'll give you the money tomorrow morning when I've been to the bank, but promise me you'll never get into that sort of trouble again."

"Okay, okay I promise" he said tetchily, "just don't nag, there's a dear."

Rupert drove Rosa to the bank in Upper Bulford first thing the following morning to withdraw the cash, even though it meant digging into the savings that provided her main income. Then, as she handed over the money to her son, she suggested having a leisurely lunch at the pub in the village, but he brushed her off, protesting that he had far too much to do, and would have to leave straight away. She quickly brushed away a tear, as she was rather hurt and disappointed that he didn't seem to have time for her, and confided as much to Jed when he called round for a cup of tea and one of her homemade cakes.

"I feel rather used; I gave him the money he asked for but he couldn't even be bothered to have lunch with me."

"Ah, you'm been too soft with him," Jed told her and then asked pointedly, "What did he want the money for, anyway?"

"Gambling debts," she replied, rolling her eyes heavenward.

"Oh Lord! Don't you go giving him no more then", Jed warned her, "that's a bottomless pit, that is! I had a cousin went down that road, and he ended up losing everything."

"Well, there won't be any more," Rosa said firmly "and he's promised not to get involved with them again." Jed didn't say anything, but he had a strong feeling that she would invariably be disappointed.

Just as he had predicted, Rosa received another phone-call from Rupert a few weeks later to tap her for more money. "Mother," he wheedled "you couldn't possibly lend me another grand, could you?"

"Whatever for this time?" asked Rosa with exasperation.

"I just had a run of bad luck, that's all, but I really need it by next week at the latest."

"I'm sorry dear," his mother sighed, "I'm afraid I just can't let you have any more."

"But I don't understand, you've still got plenty of money in your account," Rupert said in annoyance, "so why on earth won't you help me out?"

"And what am I supposed to live on, fresh air?" Rosa asked angrily. "That money only gives me a very small income Rupert, and it's not my fault if you've already squandered yours."

"Well, what am I supposed to do then?" he asked plaintively.

Rosa sighed and opened the drawer of her desk. In it lay a cheque from Lizzie for the sale of some of her paintings. She was going to use the money to buy herself some warm winter clothes, but she weakened and said, "Alright, I can let you have £250, but that's the very last time I'm going to bail you out, so don't even think of asking me for any more."

"Well, I suppose that will have to do then," he said with bad grace, and put the phone down without even thanking his mother or saying goodbye.

Rosa was very hurt by his behaviour, it was totally inexcusable, and she wondered sadly at what he had become. He had been such a dear little boy, and later she had been so proud of him when he had passed his exams to become a doctor, but lately he had changed. There was a hard, ruthless streak in him that she didn't like, and there didn't seem to be anyone special in his life at all. She would have liked nothing better than to see him settle down and maybe give her a couple of grandchildren, and she envied Jed his close and loving family.

The next time Jed came to do the garden she confided in him her disappointment in her son.

"I don't know where I've gone wrong, his father and I always gave him everything, and we were so proud when he got into medical school."

"Well, I dunno," Jed shrugged, "my two never had much as kids, and they still turned out alright. Mind you, me and the missus always spent time with 'em, and maybe that's all you can do for 'em in the end."

"My husband wasn't around that much," confessed Rosa. "He worked very hard and very long hours, but I was always there for him, and he was lovely as a little boy."

She didn't tell Jed that Leo had been constantly irritated by his son and had snapped and shouted at the poor child until he learned to keep out of his way. She supposed it was because Leo was under stress at work, but no-one could blame Rupert for trying to get his father's attention, and she reflected that perhaps the boy would have turned out differently if Leo had been able to spend more time with him.

A tear came to her eye, and she wiped it away surreptitiously, but Jed had seen it and patted her arm, saying comfortingly "Don't you go blaming yourself. He probably would have turned out the way he has whatever you done."

Rosa gave a shaky laugh and said, "Perhaps when he meets the right girl he'll change for the better."

"Let's hope so," replied Jed, although privately he didn't hold out much hope.

Chapter 14

Rosa tried to forget about Rupert and threw herself into her work. She began to paint scenes around the village, and though these sold eventually, it was the views of her cottage that flew off the walls. "I think that cottage is charmed," chuckled her friend Lizzie, "and I'm amazed that you never tire of painting it."

"I know," replied Rosa, "I'm as mystified as you. All I know is, I just love painting anything about the cottage, and I have a feeling that perhaps May has something to do with it, she's probably put a spell on me."

"Well, long may it last!" giggled Lizzie, as she placed Rosa's latest masterpiece in the window.

The local dramatic society was doing a production of A Midsummer Night's Dream up at the village hall, and Lizzie asked Rosa if she would help out with painting the scenery, and it was there that she met Jed's son for the first time. He was making up some of the screens that Rosa was to decorate with woodland scenes, and she knew immediately that he was related to Jed as he looked very like him. He had the same lean, spare frame, only he was a little taller and darker and more swarthy in his looks. He smiled shyly and introduced himself; "Hello, I'm Sam Fuller, and I'm afraid I've got a bit of a favour to ask you." Rosa was intrigued and asked him to explain.

"Well, it's Mum and Dad's Ruby wedding soon, and I wanted to give them something really special. Dad said you done some drawings of him once, and I was wondering if you could perhaps do a painting of the cottage with him working in the garden?"

"I don't see why not," Rosa said with a smile. "When would you need it by?"

Sam grimaced, "Sunday I'm afraid."

Rosa was momentarily flummoxed and said, "Oh dear, that doesn't give me very much time, especially if I've got to paint all these backdrops."

"What if I was to help with painting the screens, just the background like? It would mean such a lot to the old bugg.. sorry, the old man, and I'd pay the going rate."

Rosa grinned wickedly, "Well, we can't disappoint the old bugger, can we? You can begin painting those screens green, darker at the bottom and then gradually getting lighter towards the top, and I'll go and make a start on this painting for you."

Rosa went home and did a preliminary sketch of the cottage, placing Jed in the foreground with his scythe, and in the morning she began working on the watercolour. She worked quickly, for the day held the promise of rain, and she wanted to get most of the work done while the sun was out, so when the first raindrops fell, it was well on the way to being finished.

She presented it to Sam that evening, saying "I hope you like it, but I'm afraid I didn't have time to frame it." Sam removed the brown paper cover and gasped in amazement.

"But that's fantastic! You've got him just right, the way he stands, and his mutton chops and that old scythe of his, you can tell it's him a mile off! Thank you so much, Mum and Dad will really treasure this, now how much do I owe you?"

"Well I won't charge you too much," Rosa said, quoting him a price, "as you've got to get it framed and I know that's expensive."

"That's very good of you," said Sam gratefully, "and I hope you'll come and have a glass of wine with us on Sunday; any time between two and four."

"Oh you don't really want me there," protested Rosa, "it's a special family occasion."

"Yes of course we do," Sam insisted, "Dad will be made up to see you, and Mum's been dying to meet you for ages. Please say you'll come?"

"Alright then," smiled Rosa, "maybe just for a little while."

She had passed by Jed's house many times before, but had never been inside. It was one of three small thatched cottages in the lane leading to the church, and it was set slightly back from the road, and with a tall yew hedge at the perimeter. Jed had lived there all his life, and when his father died he had shared the house with his mother, who continued to live with him after his marriage to Nellie. His father had been gassed in the First World War, and his lungs had never fully recovered, so Jed's mother had faced a struggle to try and make ends meet.

Jed had been only four years old when his father had succumbed to a bout of influenza, and life had been very hard for him and his mother. She managed to get work in the laundry up at the Manor, and Jed accompanied her when he was not at school. He was well aware at quite a young age that he had to help to provide for them, and one of the gardeners had taken him under his wing and taught him about growing his own food. Squire Bulford also kept an eye on him and he saw to it that Jed was given the cast-off clothes and boots from his own sons.

Somehow they managed to get by, and Jed never went hungry, and as he grew older his mother came to rely on him more and more, and he often missed out on his schooling. Then, when Nellie fell pregnant and Jed had to get married, it took a while before Nellie and his mother got on but then, when the first grandchild was born, all was forgiven and the two women rubbed along fairly harmoniously for many years to come.

When Rosa knocked at the door, it was Jed himself who answered and ushered her in.

"I'm glad you're here," he told her, "Sam's being very mysterious and he won't give us his present till you arrived."

He showed her into a small, dark sitting room where the family were ranged around the walls and called his wife over, "Nellie, come and meet Rosa."

A tiny raven-haired woman extricated herself from the sofa and shook Rosa's hand, saying shyly "It's so nice to meet you at last Mrs Montford. Jed's told me a lot about you."

"Please call me Rosa, and these are for you." She handed over a fragrant bunch of red roses together with a card.

Nellie exclaimed in delight, "Ooh don't they smell lovely, and they'll go beautiful in that vase our Joanie gave us, won't they Jed?"

Nellie was the same height as Rosa, but whereas she was slender and dainty, Jed's wife resembled a little vole, round and sleek, with bright dark eyes that were imbued with merriment. Rosa could see where Sam got his colouring from, for Nellie's olive skin was tanned to a deep shade of mahogany, and her hair, dark with just a few strands of silver, lay in an untidy bun at the nape of her neck.

A woman, who Rosa supposed was Joan, got up and picked up a fancy ruby glass vase, filled it with water and then arranged the flowers, placing them on a low table. Meanwhile Sam had offered Rosa his chair, and she sat next to a pale, tired looking woman who turned out to be Sam's wife, for she leant over to thank Rosa for helping to make her daughter's costume for Midsummer Night's Dream. Just then, Sam emerged from the kitchen carrying a tray of glasses and a bottle of champagne. He popped the cork with a loud bang, which made Nellie scream, and then poured the foaming liquid into the waiting glasses.

"Can I have some, Dad?" piped a little girl who Rosa recognised as one of the fairies in the play.

Sam said, "No Kirsty, I've got some fizzy pop for you kids, and you can toast your grandparents with that."

When everybody had a glass he announced heartily, "Congratulations Mum and Dad on your Ruby wedding, and here's to the next forty years!"

"Lordy, I don't think I can stand him that long," cried Nellie, and everybody laughed, including Jed, who pinched her bottom and said loudly "You didn't say that to me in bed last night though!"

"Jed!" Nellie cried with mock indignation, and everyone laughed again, and then Sam handed over his gift. "I reckon you know what it is, don't you?"

"Yeah, but not what it's about though," replied Jed impatiently ripping off the paper and then gasping in amazement. "Why tis me, ain't it? When did you do that?" he asked Rosa in astonishment.

"Earlier this week."

"Well, tis just perfect, ain't it Nellie?"

"It's really beautiful," said Nellie in awe, and then asked "Where shall we hang it Jed, over the mantelpiece?"

"No," replied Jed emphatically, "we'll hang it over the settee, and then I can sit in me rocking chair and see what a fine figure of a man I used to be!"

"Old codger, more like," retorted Nellie, giggling as Sam hung the picture over the sofa with a flourish. He had got the painting framed in a wide, plain gold frame and that looked very fine in the room. They both kissed Sam and Rosa and thanked them for the wonderful painting, and Rosa noticed that Joan looked a little sour, as her present of the ruby vase rather paled into insignificance beside Sam's special and very personal gift.

Sam then went to turn on the record player and, putting on an album of Glen Miller, said to Jed, "How about having a little dance with Mum then?"

"You knows I can't dance," protested Jed, "you dance with her instead." Sam then pulled Nellie to her feet and whirled her round to the music, at one point lifting her right off her feet, making her scream with delight, but after a while she said, "Ooh, that's enough Sam, I'm feeling quite giddy."

She sat back down and Sam stretched out his hand to his niece, a rather sulky looking teenager dressed head to toe in black, but she shook her head, and then little Kirsty begged "Dance with me, please Daddy!"

He picked up his daughter and jigged about with her until the song ended, and then a slow number came on and he asked his wife to dance. At first she declined, saying she was too tired, but at Sam's urging she got up and he took her in his arms and she rested her head on his shoulder. As he held her he was shocked at how thin she had become, for there was hardly anything of her, and he told himself he would make her go to the doctor in the morning and not listen to any of her protests this time.

Meanwhile, Joan's husband had been sitting quietly in the corner fiddling with his cufflinks and running a finger round his too-tight shirt collar, and it was obvious that he was not used to a suit and tie, so when she pulled him up to dance he saw it as a good excuse to take off his jacket and undo his tie and collar button. Rosa thought it was time to go, but Jed wouldn't hear of it until she'd had a look around his garden.

It stretched a surprisingly long way back, and she saw that half of his neighbour's garden had also been added to his. He had planted rows of vegetables and there were several fruit bushes, and she could see a profusion of strawberry plants, and raspberry, red currant and gooseberry bushes that were laden with ripe fruit and covered by netting to keep off the birds. When she remarked on the extra land, he said, "Well, I has a very good arrangement with my neighbour. I gets to use her land in exchange for fruit and vegetables, but she lives on her own and she don't eat a great deal, so it helps me feed my crowd."

"It must be very hard work, growing all that food."

"Aye it is, but Nellie helps me out a lot. Tis a shame she ain't better at cooking it though," Jed chuckled. "Here, I'll pick you some to take home."

At the far end of the garden was a chicken coop with half a dozen hens scratching about, and Rosa said, "I didn't know you kept chickens Jed."

"Them's Nellie's hens, she's got names for 'em all. When they gets broody she lets some of the eggs hatch and sells a few of the chicks, and then the rest be replacements for when they stops laying."

He picked up one of the hens and stroked its soft feathers and Rosa asked "What happens to them then?"

"They goes in the pot o' course," replied Jed matter-of-factly.

"Isn't Nellie upset to eat her chickens, especially as she named them all?"

"Oh aye," laughed Jed, "I keeps telling her not to, but she don't listen, but she's right fond of a bit of roast chicken! Do you want a few new-laid eggs?"

"I've got enough at the moment," Rosa told him, "but I wouldn't mind some beans."

"Here, I'll pick some for you to take home."

He fetched a trug from the potting shed and then proceeded to fill it to the brim with runner beans, a few carrots and a generous selection of strawberries, raspberries and red currants, and when Rosa protested that she wouldn't be able to eat them all herself, Jed grinned at her and said cheekily, "Well, you can always make a nice fruit pie, and I'll be round on Tuesday!"

"It's a deal," laughed Rosa, and wave goodbye at the gate. As she walked slowly home, she reflected on Jed's warm and close relationship with his family. They had been so kind to her, making her feel very welcome and suddenly, for the first time, she felt a little lonely. She wondered when her son was going to get in touch again, but Rupert was always so busy and never seemed to have time for a chat, and she wondered sadly if he was ever going to make her a grandmother.

Chapter 15

Somehow the years that Rosa had spent at Honeysuckle Cottage had flown by, and her hair had now turned quite grey, but she still wore it in the same bobbed style, and it made her eyes look bigger and darker than ever. She had always been slim, but now she began to lose weight she could ill afford, and she had a persistent cough that she could not seem to shake off. It was her friend Lizzie who noticed that she was not looking well, and urged her to go see a doctor.

"Oh I'm fine, a little tired perhaps, but I'm not getting any younger," Rosa had replied airily.

Lizzie was worried and said, "You've had that cough for ages, don't you think you should give up the cigarettes?"

"I've tried a number of times," Rosa told her ruefully, "but I'm afraid I can't seem to function without them."

"Well, you really should go and see someone."

"Yes, alright, but Rupert's coming to stay next week," Rosa reassured her, "and if my cough's not gone by then, he can give me the once over."

When Rupert arrived he was really shocked by his mother's appearance. She was like a little bird, with her eyes huge in her pinched face, and with her clothes hanging off her already slender frame. He went to the car to fetch his medical bag and took out his stethoscope, and his face was grave as he listened to her chest, and he asked "How long have you had that cough?"

"Oh a while now; I can't seem to get rid of it."

"Well, I'm taking you back to London with me, and then I'll get an appointment with one of the consultants at the hospital, and I don't want to hear any excuses."

Rosa didn't want to go, but she didn't have the energy to argue with him, and since she had coughed up some blood a few days before, she felt something wasn't quite right and she should get it checked out. Rupert arranged for her to have X-rays and a thorough check-up at the hospital, and a couple of days later she went back to see the consultant Dr Chandler, who was Rupert's head of department.

He looked grave as he asked her to sit down. "I'm afraid it's rather serious, Mrs Montford, as you have a tumour on the right lung, and also two smaller ones on the left, and it also appears to have spread into your duodenum. There may possibly be others that we haven't spotted, but I'm afraid the prognosis isn't good. We can try chemotherapy and radiotherapy, but in my opinion the cancer is rather too far advanced for the treatment to be successful."

Rosa was stunned, she had not expected that her illness was that serious, and it took her a few moments to take in what the consultant had told her. Then she asked "What if I decide not to have the treatment, how long have I got?"

"A few months at the most, I'm afraid."

"Thank you, I need to think about this, and talk it over with my son." Rosa sat quietly for a moment, allowing the dreadful news to sink in, and then asked, "What would be my chances of a full recovery if I have the treatment?"

Doctor Chandler hesitated for a moment before replying, "In my opinion, about 25 per cent. I'm so sorry Mrs Montford, but if you had come to us sooner, the prognosis would have been far more optimistic."

Rupert's eyes had filled with tears when she told him, and he begged her to have treatment, but she had made up her mind not to put herself through that gruelling ordeal for the sake of a few more months, especially as the odds were so stacked against her. She wanted to continue to paint and savour her life at the cottage for as long as possible, and then, when the time came, she would have to sell it to pay for her nursing care at the end.

Jed Fuller was the first person she told that she had terminal cancer. They had a comfortable friendship, and she didn't know how she would have ever managed without him. He was devastated when she told him the news, although he had tried not to let her see it, for he had not expected that. He had known that she was ill, but had thought it was merely a bad lung infection, and that she would recover with a course of antibiotics.

Jed had grown very fond of Rosa, although at first he had been a little wary of her. She spoke with what he considered to be a posh accent, and was obviously very well-educated, but to her credit she had always treated him as an equal, and had never talked down to him. He admired her and thought that she had taken the news very bravely, but he was going to miss her terribly, and now she confided, "I'm afraid I'm going to have to sell Honeysuckle Cottage to pay for my care Jed, but I don't want to leave it until the last minute. There's going to be such a lot to do and I want to get everything sorted while I'm still able to."

He had patted her arm and replied reassuringly, "Well, no doubt something will turn up. Don't you be a worrying, as I reckons these things always work out when there's a real need."

"Yes, you're probably right," sighed Rosa, "but I don't want to sell it to someone who would change the cottage. It's really such a special and unique building, and it would break my heart if it were to be ruined."

"Aye, that would be a shame," agreed Jed, "and I don't reckon May would be too happy neither." They laughed at that, and Rosa wondered what she would do if someone tried to change Honeysuckle Cottage. "Probably scare the living daylights out of 'em," chuckled Jed, but in the end it all worked out rather well.

DAMIAN

Chapter 16

The phone was ringing continuously, and as Damian Shaw picked it up he cursed silently. It was Deborah Miller, his literary agent, and she was bending his ear about his latest book, or rather, the lack of it. "You promised me the first two chapters last week Damian," she screeched, "and I'm still waiting. It's just not good enough, is it?" Now, when can I expect them?"

"Yes, I'm really sorry Debs," he said in a patient, long-suffering voice that drove her mad, "but I'm having a bit of trouble with my computer. I'm just waiting for a chap to come and fix it, but I'm sure I'll be able to get them to you by the end of next week."

It was a blatant lie, there was nothing wrong with the computer; he simply hadn't written a single word of his book. He had found Debbie rather intimidating the first time he had met her. It wasn't just her size, which was generous to say the least, but she had a loud and bombastic manner which in truth hid a rather shy personality, but he soon realised that she had a heart of gold and that she really nurtured her clients.

The truth was that Damian had hit a dry patch, and the ideas just wouldn't come. It didn't help that he'd been having a busy social life, and the late nights meant that he didn't get up until noon and then, what with wine fuelled lunches and his afternoon naps, there wasn't a great deal of time left for writing. He sighed, and realised that he would have to do something pretty soon though, or his money would run out.

As if she'd read his mind, his agent said, "I've booked you on a two-day seminar Damian, and it will mean giving a talk and answering questions about your books, and of course the usual book signings, and its next weekend, don't let me down."

"What, where?" asked Damian in alarm, for he hated giving talks.

"It's at the Bulford Manor Hotel in Lower Bulford," Debbie told him. "The money's not brilliant, but hopefully you can sell a few books, and it'll keep you in the public eye till your new book comes out."

Damian drove up to Bulford Manor in a foul mood for he hated doing these lecture tours, and this place was so far out in the sticks that he'd never even heard of it, and he had to stop and check his map a couple of times on the way. Once he'd arrived he had to admit it was a pretty village though, and the pub, The Bulford Arms, looked welcoming, and he resolved to go and have a drink there the following day.

The lecture went better than he'd expected as he had made the audience laugh a few times, and he'd also managed to sell a couple of dozen books. Not as many as he'd hoped, but it was better than nothing. The next day was sunny and fresh, and he decided to go for a brisk walk before treating himself to lunch at the pub, and then having to face the long drive back to London. On his wanderings through the village he saw the tea-rooms cum art gallery, and on the spur of the moment went in.

As he entered he noticed a small bird-like woman who was in earnest conversation with a large blonde woman who turned out to be the proprietor, for she hurried over and asked what she could get him.

"Actually, I just came in to look at the paintings," Damian confessed, "would that be alright?"

"Yes, of course," replied Lizzie Appleby, "they're all for sale, and we have a lovely selection of cards as well," she added with a smile.

As he looked at the varying pieces of artwork, there was one that drew him back. It was a watercolour of a cottage, the porch covered in cascading honeysuckle, and the garden bright with flowers, and he asked "How much is this one? I think it's really lovely."

"That one is £150, and this happens to be the artist," said the owner pointing to the bird-like woman who smiled, saying "Hello, I'm Rosa Montford, and you're Damian Shaw aren't you?"

"Yes, were you at the lecture at the manor? I'm afraid I didn't notice you."

"No," she replied "but I've read all your books, and your photo on the book jacket is a good likeness." She smiled, and he noticed her large, dark eyes and thought she must have been very beautiful in her youth.

"I'll take the painting; it'll cheer up my gloomy London flat. Was it painted locally?"

"Yes, actually it's my own cottage," said Rosa. "Would you like to come and see it?"

"I'd love to," replied Damian eagerly, "do you have time now?"

Rosa told him she had all the time in the world and, once the painting was wrapped and paid for, she led the way to her cottage. More than once she had to stop and catch her breath, and Damian asked with concern if he should go and get his car, but she shook her head. "No, I'm fine and we're almost there now. I'm sorry about all the stops, but my lungs are bad, so I have to pace myself."

Once they had rounded the corner and Honeysuckle Cottage came into view, Damian was enthusiastic with his praise. "Oh what a darling little cottage, it's exactly like your painting, you are so lucky to live here."

"Yes, I've been very blessed." Rosa smiled gently, "Now I'll put the kettle on while you have a look round."

Opening the door to the sitting room Damian exclaimed "What a fabulous window! Is this where you do your painting?"

"Yes, mostly when it's wet or too cold to go out, the light is amazing, isn't it?"

"I'll say! It must be wonderful to work there." He could just picture himself sitting there at his desk, and suddenly the thought of no distractions seemed very appealing, and he knew that here he would be able to knuckle down to some serious work.

"May I go and look upstairs?" he asked Rosa, who said yes and then asked if he preferred tea or coffee. "Coffee please, milk no sugar, I have to watch the old waistline." He went up to Rosa's bedroom where the view of the garden was enchanting. It was a real old-fashioned cottage garden, and he imagined himself waking up here to the birds singing instead of the noise of traffic, with the air smelling of roses and honeysuckle instead of petrol fumes.

When he went back down Rosa had made the coffee and was setting out some homemade biscuits. "How nice, I can't remember the last time I ate something homemade." Damian told her and sat down at the scrubbed pine table and slowly sipped his coffee. "I don't suppose you would consider ever selling this place, would you?" he asked hopefully.

"As it happens, yes, and I'm afraid I need a quick sale," Rosa told him sadly. "I haven't got much time left, and I will need to go into a nursing home soon."

"I'm so sorry, I had no idea."

"No reason why you should," smiled Rosa. "In fact, I think you were heaven sent!"

"Now that's something no-one's ever said to me before," quipped Damian.

She added a proviso and told him "If I do sell you the cottage, there are a couple of conditions."

Damian looked a little perturbed and asked, "What sort of conditions?"

"Firstly, that you allow me to stay on here till I have to go into a hospice..."

"Of course," said Damian quickly, "that goes without saying."

"The other condition is that you don't alter the structure of the house in any way, no new wings added or new windows put in. I'm trying to get the house listed, as it's so unusual."

"Oh I wouldn't want to change a thing," he reassured her, "it's perfect just as it is."

Rosa was relieved to hear that, but she said, "However, there is something else you need to know, the cottage has a ghost."

Damian laughed delightedly, "But that's great, as long as it's a friendly ghost?"

"Yes, she's very friendly; in fact, I've found her quite a comforting presence."

Damian leaned back and asked, "Now tell me the bad news, how much is this little corner of paradise going to cost me?"

"Well, I haven't really thought. I ought to get some idea from the local estate agents," Rosa said but reassured him "but you can be sure I won't be greedy. All I want is enough to pay for my care and my funeral, and to be sure this house is going to someone who'll love and look after it."

Damian assured her he would, and to seal their bargain offered to treat her to lunch at the Bulford Arms. Rosa accepted and was grateful when he offered to fetch the car, showing him a short cut to get to the manor from the lane, and over lunch she told him all about May and the history of the cottage as she knew it. Damian ate heartily, and Rosa watched him with approval, but she merely picked at her food, as she didn't have much of an appetite lately, but she still managed to enjoy a nice glass of wine.

"It seems strange that those amazing windows were put into a humble woodcutter's cottage," said Damian as they were drinking their coffee.

Rosa nodded and said, "Yes, it is rather odd, but you should really speak to Jed Fuller. He's my gardener and he was a friend to May, and he knows a lot more about the history of the area than I do."

After lunch, Damian drove Rosa back to the cottage, and they agreed that once she had worked out a price, she would telephone him and, if he could afford to buy, they would do all the paperwork the following weekend.

On the drive home Damian was in a very happy mood and began to get an idea for his next book. He had been fascinated and touched by the story of May, and congratulated himself on the good fortune that had led him to meet Rosa and see quirky Honeysuckle Cottage.

Rosa was as good as her word and phoned him the following Tuesday. He had almost not answered the phone, fearing it was Debbie, his agent, about to shout at him again, but at the last minute he picked it up to hear her say, "Damian? This is Rosa."

"Oh Rosa, hi," he said relieved, "how are you feeling?"

"Not too bad thanks. Now, I've spoken to the agents and they valued my cottage at £65,000..." There was a sharp intake of breath at Damian's end, and she quickly added "...but don't panic, I'm not asking that much. How does £35,000 sound?"

"Much better," he said with relief. "I think we have a deal, but I need to have a word with my bank manager first, and I'll ring you in a couple of days."

He made an appointment with his bank, as in order to buy the cottage he would have to re-mortgage his flat in Chelsea, but he didn't think that would be a problem, and he could rent out the flat to cover the repayments, and live on his savings while he wrote the new book.

When he called at the bank and told the manager why he wanted to borrow the money, the manager was a little sniffy at first, and said, "I don't know why it has to be done in such a hurry Mr Shaw, why can't you go through proper channels with the mortgage company?"

"I haven't got time," Damian told him, "the lady that's selling the cottage is dying and needs to go into a nursing home fairly soon, and I don't want to lose the cottage."

"I see, and how much would you need to borrow?"

"I'm afraid I need the full amount of £35,000, but it really is a bargain, as the agents have valued it at nearly twice that."

"Oh really?" The manager suddenly became far more amenable. "Well, Mr Shaw, if you can provide me with proof of its value, I think we can do business."

Damian rushed home and phoned Rosa excitedly. "Rosa, I think the bank manager is going to give me the loan, but he needs the valuation of the cottage from the estate agents. Could you send it to me as soon as possible?"

"Of course, I'll put it in the post today. Will he lend you the full amount?"

"Yes, and it's only until I sort it out with the mortgage people, but I'll call you as soon as I've got the money."

While he was in a good mood he decided to take the bull by the horns and phone his agent. "Hi Debs, its Damian…"

"At last! I've been trying to call you for days," she said crossly, "where the hell are those chapters you promised?"

"Sorry, but something much more exiting came up. Look, how about I take you out for lunch tomorrow and tell you all about it?"

They had agreed to meet in Soho at the historic Rules restaurant, and when Damian arrived Debbie was already there, wedged into a corner table. She heaved her bulky figure out of the seat with difficulty and gave him a peck on both cheeks before saying, "I should really give you a good shaking, where on earth have you been?"

"Well, you know I gave that talk at Bulford Manor?"

Debbie nodded, "Yes, but that was days ago."

"I know, but I met this really interesting lady. She's an artist, and she lives in the most delightful gothic cottage in the woods and..."

"But what has all this got to do with your book?"

"I'm coming to that, if you'll stop interrupting," Damian said and continued "anyway, this lady is dying, and she needs to sell the cottage quickly, and so I've decided to buy it."

"What, just like that? Are you mad?" Debbie looked at him askance. "You're going to hide yourself away in the middle of nowhere on a whim?"

"Well, if you put it like that, it does sound mad, but you haven't seen the cottage. It's so quaint, and best of all, it has a ghost."

"What utter rubbish! Damian you amaze me sometimes."

"It's true," he protested, "Rosa's often felt her presence. Her name was May, and she lived in the cottage years ago and had a really tragic life. In fact, I'm going to write her story, but I need to do more research, so it makes perfect sense to live there, doesn't it?"

"And what about the book you're working on now?"

"Oh that wasn't going anywhere," Damian said airily. "I've binned it for the time being. Now just wait till I tell you all about May."

After a hearty lunch and a couple of bottles of wine, Damian persuaded Debbie to give him a few weeks' grace. She had been touched by the story of May and agreed that it sounded a much better prospect than the one he had supposedly been working on.

By the end of the week Damian had the money for the cottage and phoned Rosa straight away to give her the good tidings. "That's wonderful news!" she said with relief, as she had feared that he might have difficulty in borrowing such a large amount. "I'll have a legal agreement drawn up over the next couple of days, so why don't you come down on Friday? And stay the weekend if you'd like to."

"Oh that's very kind of you, but I really don't want to put you to any trouble," he protested. "I can stay the night at the pub."

"Nonsense!" Rosa said firmly. "It's as good as your cottage now anyway, and it's no trouble to me, and besides, I want you to meet Jed Fuller because he knows everything about May."

When Damian arrived at the cottage he was struck by how ill Rosa looked. She was very pale with dark shadows under her eyes, and even thinner if that were possible, but her face lit up when she saw him. He had brought a bottle of wine and an expensive bunch of flowers, and Rosa was thrilled with the bouquet. "How lovely, I adore flowers. I'll have to try and paint them before they fade." She had some meat and vegetables roasting in the oven, and Damian breathed in the aroma hungrily, but before they sat down to eat Rosa gave him the agreement to peruse.

It stated that she would be allowed to stay in the cottage for up to three months from the date of signing, and that the cottage was not to be structurally altered in any way. "I've applied for a grade two listed status on the cottage," she told him, "it should come through fairly soon. Don't worry about the three months, as realistically I think it will only be about two or three weeks."

"As soon as that?" asked Damian with concern.

"Yes, I've been feeling very tired and not very well lately, and it's only going to get worse."

They sat down to eat, with Damian tucking in hungrily, but Rosa merely picked at her food. She said, "I've asked Jed to pop in later for a cup of tea. I don't know if you'll want to keep him on as a gardener, but he's very useful, providing logs for the range, and any odd jobs that need doing around the place."

Jed arrived promptly at four, and brought Rosa a marrow and some tomatoes from his greenhouse. Damian smiled and shook hands and thought what a marvellous character he would make in one of his stories, and Rosa introduced them "Mr Shaw's a famous writer Jed, and he's going to buy my cottage."

"How do, you from London then?" asked Jed, holding out a grubby hand, and when Damian nodded, he said, "I reckon you'll find it a bit too quiet around here like."

"Actually, it's the peace and quiet I need," Damian told him. "I can't seem to get down to any work in London and I think this place would be perfect. Rosa tells me you used to know May, and I was wondering if you could tell me something about her."

"What do you want to know?"

"Everything."

It took three cups of tea and several biscuits for Jed to get the whole of his tale told, and Rosa excused herself, saying she needed a bit of a lie down. When Jed finally left, Damian said, "I do hope you'll still come and do the garden for me and show me the ropes. As you've probably guessed, I'm a bit of a novice when it comes to country matters."

"Oh aye, I'll be glad to. Two days a week suit? Same rates as Rosa pays me," and as an afterthought he added, "oh, and I likes me cup of tea in the afternoon."

When he had gone Damian decided he would wash-up the lunch and tea things. It was the least he could do for Rosa after such a splendid meal, and she was pleasantly surprised when she came downstairs.

"Oh you shouldn't have done that, you're my guest. Now, what did you think of Jed?"

"He's such an amazing character, I could listen to him for hours."

Rosa laughed, "You'll probably regret saying that. He can talk for England once he gets going, and he'll charge you for the privilege."

They turned in early, and Damian made a few notes on the conversation he'd had with Jed and he reflected how sad it was that May had felt the need to hide herself away, as these days they could have done marvels with plastic surgery, and she would have been able to lead a normal life. He yawned sleepily, but once he got into bed he found it very hard to get to sleep. He could hear Rosa coughing incessantly in the other room, and began to wish he'd done what he intended and taken a room at the pub.

After breakfast the following morning, Damian signed the agreement and paid Rosa the money and she handed him the deeds. "I don't know if you want the furniture, most of it came with the cottage, but I don't think Rupert will want to take much."

"Sorry, but who's Rupert?"

"Oh, didn't I mention him? He's my son."

"Actually, I would like the furniture," Damian told her "as I'm going to rent out my London flat, so it will save me having to buy new stuff. Do you want some more money for it?" he asked anxiously.

Rosa shook her head. "No, I'm just glad it's of use, and now here are the keys and the cottage is officially yours!"

Damian wanted to take her out to lunch to celebrate, but she declined, saying she was too tired and in quite a bit of pain, and she needed to sort out some papers. "I'll give the spare keys to Jed when I leave, and I'll ring you as soon as I know when I'm going."

A couple of weeks later he got a call from Rosa to tell him she was going into a hospice. Damian was shocked and said with concern, "I'm sorry it's so soon, would you like me to come and see you?"

"Yes, that would be kind. Jed knows where I'll be, and my son is going to clear out my things the day after tomorrow, so you can move in any time after that."

Chapter 17

Rupert had taken a couple of days off work in order to move Rosa into the hospice. There wasn't much to pack, for as Rosa had said, "I'm dying, so none of it's any use to me now." She took a small suitcase of clothing, a couple of framed photographs and her favourite vase. "Jed's sure to bring me some flowers," she told him "and I need something to put them in. I've told Damian he can have any of the furniture and household bits that you don't want, and you can take my clothes down to Oxfam..." She paused, wracked by a coughing fit, and when she had regained her breath, continued, "...and I've already thrown away all the worn items and the underwear, so what's left is still usable."

The hospice was an annex of the general hospital at Upper Bulford. It was set a little apart from the main building, and Rosa's room, which was on the ground floor overlooking a formal garden, had been freshly painted and had a pretty chintz bedcover and curtains. "We try to make it homely for our patients," the nurse explained as she showed Rosa into her room which also had a small bathroom attached, "we don't want people to end their days in a bleak ward." Rupert took his leave and said, "I'll come and see you tomorrow Mother, and if you've forgotten anything call me at the cottage, and I'll bring it with me."

He had been furious when his mother told him she had sold the cottage, but he could not let her see the way he felt. "I've had to sell it to pay for my care darling," she had explained, "but whatever's left, after my funeral expenses, is yours; the solicitor has a copy of my will, and he'll contact you." The cottage seemed strange without her presence, but it was imbued with her personality, and as Rupert looked around he could see very little that he wanted apart from a few photographs, but he would take anything that was easily saleable.

There was a watercolour hanging over the fireplace that Rosa had painted from a photograph, and it was of himself aged about six or seven, dressed in a smart school uniform and clutching a teddy bear. He had hated that school, and had begged his parents to let him stay at the local one where all his friends were, but his end of term report had said that he was disruptive in class and was not paying enough attention to his lessons. His father had been furious, and had insisted that he be sent to a private school where he didn't know anyone, and where he would be forced to concentrate on his school work.

Rosa had tried to stand up for him, but his father had told her it was for his own good and then she had reluctantly agreed, and ignoring his tears and pleading, marched him off so that they could catch the bus to take him to his new school. He had hated his father then, and despised his mother for not being strong enough to stand up to him. He clearly remembered her taking his photo in his new uniform, and refusing to smile to please her, and all the old feelings of impotent anger and hurt came flooding back, and in a sudden fit of rage he snatched the painting from the wall and stamped hard on it, shattering the glass into a dozen pieces.

His mother's easel was set up by the window, a watercolour of the garden still pinned to it, and there was another rolled up on the table. He decided he would take them down to the little art gallery in the village and get some money for them; likewise with her paints and easel. There was a second-hand shop in Upper Bulford that might give him a few quid for them.

He went upstairs and began to empty the wardrobe and chest of drawers of her clothes, putting them into black sacks ready to take to the charity shop in the morning. Her jewel box stood on top of the chest, and he opened it and saw a gold locket that he had seen her wear many times before. It contained a picture of himself aged about five and, in a sentimental moment, he slipped it into his pocket but the rest of the jewellery he would sell for as much as he could get.

The scent of honeysuckle in the room was suddenly overwhelming and very cloying, and he felt that he couldn't breathe, and he couldn't wait to get out of the house. He grabbed another black bag and swept the chest of drawers clear of all her make-up, pills and potions, and then did the same with the bathroom cabinet. Looking at the wrought iron bed he thought it was a shame that it was too big to fit into his car. They were fetching a lot of money in London, but it would probably cost more to transport than the bed was worth, so reluctantly he decided to leave it where it was.

Carrying the sacks downstairs, he looked around the rooms again, but there was nothing he wanted apart from a pair of rather fine marble book-ends that he had given her as a house warming gift. As he removed them, a book fell to the floor and he saw that it was by Damian Shaw, and he mused, wasn't he the chap that had bought the cottage? He decided to load the car in the morning and, as his stomach was rumbling, took himself down to the pub for a bite to eat.

That night was one of those hot, sweltering nights with not even a hint of a breeze, and as Rupert attempted to sleep in Rosa's bed, the scent of honeysuckle was overpowering, and he got up to close the window. The room then became too hot and stuffy, and he tossed and turned but reluctantly had to open the window again. Covering his face with the sheet, he eventually managed to drift off to sleep.

A sudden crash woke him with a start, and his heart began pounding and he thought that there was an intruder in the house. He went downstairs to check, but the house was quiet, and he chided himself for being fanciful, but then he noticed that his photograph, which had been standing on the bookcase at the side of the fireplace, was now on the floor across the room, the glass shattered. It looked as though it had been thrown with some force, but there was no sign of a break-in.

The hairs on the back of his neck prickled, and he remembered that his mother had told him that the house was haunted, but he didn't believe in ghosts, yet could find no explanation for what had occurred. There seemed to be a dark shadow in one corner of the room, and as he went to investigate the air suddenly became icy and he shivered in apprehension, but there was nothing there, so why did he have this feeling of fear?

The incident had disturbed him far more than he would have admitted, but he went back to bed and attempted to sleep once more. He heard the church clock strike three, and then he must have fallen asleep because he dreamt that the honeysuckle was creeping across the bed and wrapping around his throat, and a heavy weight was pressing on his chest, making it harder and harder to breathe.

He woke with a start, and seemed to see a dark figure on the bed and, fumbling for the unfamiliar light switch, he turned on the bedside lamp and immediately the dark shape vanished along with the pressure on his chest. The sheet had managed to wrap around his throat, accounting for the feeling of being strangled, but he could not explain the other sensation.

It was starting to grow light when he fell into an exhausted sleep, but the broken night meant that he was not in the best of moods the following morning, and as he made himself a strong cup of coffee, he noticed two folders lying on the kitchen table.

One folder was marked Damian, and contained bills from the electricity, water and phone companies, with a reminder to change them into his name, and wishing him all the best in his new home. The other folder contained Rosa's personal paperwork, her passport, bank statements, her address book and also a valuation of the cottage from the estate agents for £65,000. He whistled appreciatively, for there would be a tidy sum left over for him once she had passed away. Out of interest, he looked at her bank book, just to see if Damian had paid the full price, but the amount entered was only £35,000. He was puzzled and couldn't understand what had happened, unless Damian had only paid her half, the rest payable when he moved in.

Later, as he was loading up the car, Jed turned up to see if he needed any help with moving his stuff. "No, I'm alright thanks," Rupert said, then asked curiously "by the way, is it Damian Shaw the writer that's bought the cottage?"

"Aye, that's right."

"Well, do you happen to know when he'll be paying the rest of the money?"

Jed looked puzzled and said, "But he's already paid. Rosa's got all the money and he's got the deeds and the keys; the cottage is his all legal like."

"But that's outrageous! He's only paid about half the value."

"Aye, I knows, but there was an agreement made between him and Rosa."

"What agreement?" Rupert asked furiously.

Jed just shrugged and said in an off-hand manner "I wouldn't know nothing 'bout that, you'll have to ask Rosa."

Rupert drove off with a squeal of tyres, having thrust the keys angrily at Jed. He stopped at the art gallery and introduced himself stiffly to Lizzie.

"Good morning, I'm Dr Montford, Rosa's son, and I've got a couple of my mother's watercolours that you might be interested in purchasing."

Lizzie unrolled them and exclaimed "But they're lovely! Don't you want to keep them as a memento of her?"

Rupert shook his head and said, "They're a bit twee for my liking. How much will you give me for them?"

Lizzie bit her lip, as she thought him rude and obnoxious, but said, "Well, as they haven't been framed, about £50 for the two."

"That's fine," he said curtly, and she opened the till and handed him the money thinking how sad it was that he did not seem to appreciate his mother's talent.

In Upper Bulford he dropped the black sacks of clothes at Oxfam, and then headed for the second-hand shop. The owner was very interested in the jewellery, but didn't particularly want the easel or artist's materials, but Rupert was not in the mood to be messed about with, so said tartly that they came as a package, take it or leave it. The man decided to take it, handing over £150 in ten pound notes.

On the drive over to the hospice Rupert was fuming, but when he saw Rosa looking so small and frail, all his anger just melted away. He decided she had been the victim of a con trick, and later asked her why she had sold the cottage so cheaply. Rosa replied, "It was an arrangement I made with Damian."

"But why? You could have got much more for it."

"I know, Rupert dear," she said gently, "but Damian loved Honeysuckle Cottage as much as I did, and I don't need the money."

"But what about me?" he asked petulantly.

She smiled ruefully and said, "You would have sold it for as much as you could get regardless, wouldn't you?"

"True," he answered, "but why would that matter?"

"Oh Rupert," she said sadly, knowing that he would never understand, "money isn't everything."

Soon it was time to say goodbye, and they both wept a little, knowing that in all probability they would not see each other again. On the drive back to London Rupert mulled over and over in his mind the fact that he'd been cheated out of his rightful inheritance, and resolved to do something about it.

Chapter 18

Damian was quite sad about Rosa, for he had grown rather fond of her, but he was excited about moving into the cottage, and began to pack up his things and get the flat ready to be rented out. He dropped the keys into the estate agents the following day, and was surprised when the doorbell rang about nine o'clock that evening.

A tall dark-haired man stood on the threshold and asked, "Are you Damian Shaw?"

"Yes," Damian replied, "but I didn't think the agents would send anyone so soon."

"I'm not from the agents. I'm Doctor Montford, and I want a word with you."

"I'm sorry, what about?" asked Damian nervously, for alarm bells were ringing and the man did not look friendly.

"It concerns my mother," and when Damian looked blank he added, "Rosa Montford, my mother?"

"Oh, you must be Rupert, please come in, how is she?"

"Not very well," replied Rupert gruffly.

He entered the flat then turned sharply to Damian, towering over him, and said, "Now I want to know how you conned her out of that cottage."

"Excuse me?" said Damian indignantly, "I paid your mother the amount she asked for and I certainly did not con her in any way."

"Do you deny that you only paid her half the value of the cottage?"

"That's between Rosa and me," said Damian in annoyance. "She quoted me a price and I paid it, and she certainly knew the value of the cottage, but it was her choice to sell it to me for less."

"Why, what did you say to her, did you threaten her?" Rupert Montford was leaning over Damian in a very antagonistic way and Damian, fearing he was going to be thumped, dodged behind the sofa.

"I most definitely did not threaten your mother," Damian said with indignation, "the idea is ludicrous; she's my friend. Now you'd better go, or I'll call the police."

"Alright, I'm going," Rupert muttered, "but you've not heard the last of this."

When Rupert Montford had gone, Damian locked the door and poured himself a stiff drink. It had shaken and upset him to think that he could be thought capable of intimidating a sick woman. Rosa had her own agenda, and she wanted the cottage to be loved and cared for, something that she obviously thought her son would not do. She also needed a quick sale to pay for her care at the end of her life, something else that her son could not, or would not, do for her. He knew he had nothing to reproach himself for, but convincing Rosa's son was not going to be so easy.

The agents managed to find him a tenant by the end of the week, so without further ado Damian packed up his things and moved into Honeysuckle Cottage. He had phoned Jed Fuller to let him know he was coming, and when he arrived he found that Jed had lit the range and stocked up a good supply of logs. He turned up later that afternoon offering his help should it be needed, but Damian had already shifted the only piece of furniture he'd brought, his writing desk, which he had positioned in front of the large window.

Damian made a pot of tea and, like Rosa before him, sat at the kitchen table and talked to Jed about his future plans. He wanted to keep everything exactly as it was when Rosa had been there, which suited Jed perfectly, and as long as he had somewhere pleasant to sit with a glass of wine, he could do what he liked in the garden. Jed asked hopefully if he had any biscuits, and Damian managed to dig out a packet of Rich Tea. Jed sighed and said wistfully "I must say, I do miss Rosa's cakes, she was a right good cook."

"How is she?" asked Damian with concern.

"Not too good, I don't reckon she'll last much longer," Jed replied.

"Do you think she'd like me to visit her?"

"I'm sure she'd be right glad to see you," Jed told him, "she thought quite a lot of you."

Damian told Jed about the unpleasant visit from Doctor Montford, but Jed reassured him and said, "Don't you take no notice of him, he's all talk. He's just miffed she didn't leave him the cottage, but she knew he didn't really want it. He would have just sold it on for as much as he could get, and she wanted it to go to someone who'd look after it." He sniffed loudly and added, "and he hardly ever came to see her, even when he knew she was so ill."

"I suppose as a doctor he is a busy man, but he was very threatening."

"Well, there ain't nothing he can do, it's all legal and it's what Rosa wanted."

Damian went to visit Rosa the following day. He had picked her a large bunch of roses and honeysuckle from the cottage garden, thinking it would cheer her up to have a reminder of her old home. She was waiting for him in the conservatory, but he was shocked by her appearance as seemed to have shrunken into herself, with her skin an unhealthy-looking parchment colour, and she frequently had to use an oxygen cylinder to aid her breathing. However, she smiled broadly, obviously pleased that he had come to see her, and she was delighted with the flowers.

"How thoughtful of you Damian, when I smell their scent I can imagine I'm back in my garden. Are you settling in alright?"

"Yes, Jed had the range going, and we had a good chat over a cup of tea, but he says he misses your cakes." Rosa laughed, then had a coughing fit and apologised.

"Sorry Damian. Yes that certainly sounds like Jed; you'll have to learn to bake if you want to get into his good books."

Damian wondered if he should say anything about Rupert's visit, but then decided not to, as he didn't want to upset Rosa but, as if she had read his mind, she asked "Has my son been to see you by any chance?"

"Yes," he said ruefully "he did call round."

"I hope he wasn't too rude, he can be a bit overbearing sometimes," Rosa admitted. "He takes after his father in that respect, but take no notice of anything he might say. I wanted you to have the cottage, and it's all legal and above board, so he can huff and puff, but he won't be able to do anything about it."

"Thanks, Rosa, you can rest assured I'll look after it," Damian reassured her, "and I promise I won't change a thing."

"That's good. Now forgive me Damian, I need to have lie down."

"Are you in pain?" he asked solicitously, but she smiled and said, "No, just very weary."

He would never see her again, for Rosa passed away in her sleep three days later. Damian attended the funeral with Jed, and amongst Rosa's friends from the village were a couple of her London friends, and of course her son. Damian tried hard to avoid him, but he made a point of coming over and hissing a warning that he'd not heard the last of him.

Chapter 19

Damian got into a routine of work. He would write for three hours every morning, walk down to the pub for lunch and then, after a snooze in the afternoon, would write for another hour or so. On the afternoons that Jed came however, his routine changed, for then a lot of tea was drunk, and he would be brought up to date with all the goings on in the village, for he loved to gossip just as much as Jed. The old man often reminisced about the old days, and told Damian about an incident from his schooldays that made him roar with laughter.

He and another boy had spent their playtimes painstakingly scratching away the limestone filler between the bricks in the boy's lavatory, until finally they were able to remove the brick andsee into the girl's toilet.

"When the brick was put back, it left a big enough gap so we could see the girls pull their knickers down," chuckled Jed, "and me and me mate used to take it in turns to spy on the girls."

"Didn't they twig?" asked Damian. "Not at first, no, but May gave me my come-uppance," Jed replied.

"How did she do that then?"

"Well me and me mate were both right sweet on her, so we was squabbling over who got to look through the crack, and she must have heard us and seen the gap. Well, the next time I took a look at her she puffed a load of chalk dust through the hole; went straight in me eye it did, and I come roaring out the toilets, me face as white as snow and me eye red and weeping from the chalk." He chuckled at the memory, and said, "I got a good leathering from the teacher, but it were worth it to see what she had under her frock."

"You dirty devil!" laughed Damian delightedly.

Jed just shrugged and said, "There weren't no sex education in them days see, we had to find things out for ourselves."

Most weekends one or two of Damian's London friends would come down and stay overnight, and then followed an exploration of all the public houses in the area. All his friends thought he was mad to bury himself in the country, and tried hard to persuade him to come back to the city, but he was managing to write, and the book was coming on well. There was one thing that puzzled him however, as he had obtained copies of May's birth and death certificates, but the cause of her death did not seem to tally with what Jed had told him.

He had said to Damian that May had died because her lungs had haemorrhaged, so the next time that the old man came to the cottage he showed him the certificate and asked "What do you make of this Jed?" Jed looked it over, but the letters kept jumping about on the page and he could not make head or tail of it, but he would never have admitted in a million years that he could not read or write, so after a moment he shrugged and handed it back to Damian who asked, "Do you think it's a mistake then?"

"Aye, I reckon," replied Jed and then quickly changed the subject, asking Damian if he was happy with the garden and what vegetables he was planning to grow.

One dull morning, when the mist was so thick he could not see to the end of his garden, Damian was writing at his desk when he felt an icy chill at his back and a feeling as if someone was standing behind him. Turning quickly, he realised there was no-one there, but the hairs on the back of his neck began to prickle, and suddenly the papers on the desk rustled as if blown by a gentle breeze although the window was tightly shut. One of the papers slid to the floor, and as he bent to retrieve it, he saw a piece of card wedged between the floorboards and something compelled him to take his paper-knife and winkle it out carefully.

It was an old sepia photograph of a young woman and, judging by the clothes, it dated from the 1930s. "Is this you May?" he asked softly, and then felt the lightest touch on the top of his head before the room returned to normal, and he put the photo safely into his desk drawer to show to Jed the next time he came round.

"Oh yes, that's May alright!" exclaimed Jed when he was shown the photo. "I reckon that were took about 1937, she'd have been about seventeen, and right pretty she was too." Damian told Jed what had happened, and the old man chuckled, "I reckon she wanted you to find that picture, and she seems to like what you're doing. Perhaps she wants you to put it into the book."

"Yes, it would look great on the cover," agreed Damian, "I'll keep it safe and show it to my agent when she comes down."

Damian had felt obliged to invite Debbie down for the following weekend, as she had been dropping heavy hints, wanting to know what the cottage was like. She had been very positive about his first three chapters, and told him that in her opinion it was the best thing he'd written so far, and when she arrived she was also very enthusiastic over the cottage.

"It's absolutely darling!" she had cried, "I can see why you fell in love with it."

He had watched her stagger up the path with two loaded carrier bags stamped with the name of a well-known Greek delicatessen, and she boomed "I come bearing gifts!"

"I can see that," he said delightedly, relieving her of one of the bags and beginning to unpack the contents. He pulled out some pitta bread, a pot of hummus, some taramasalata, feta cheese, a large jar of olives, and to wash it all down, a couple of bottles of good red wine.

"I thought I'd give you a taste of what you're missing," she said cheerfully. "I don't suppose you can get foreign food out here in the sticks?"

She took some pasturma sausages from her bag and Damian rubbed his hands in glee, saying "Oh they're my favourites."

Debbie then produced a large pot of Greek yoghurt, some small cucumbers and a clove of garlic, and then swore. "Damn, I was going to make you tsatsiki, but I've forgotten the mint."

"There's plenty in the vegetable patch," Damian replied, and then set the table for lunch out in the garden, as it was still warm enough to sit outside, and they tucked into the Greek feast surrounded by sweet-smelling honeysuckle and roses.

"Oh, that was heaven, thank you Debs," said Damian, rubbing his bulging stomach and relaxing back in his chair, "I couldn't eat another thing; it's so good to have something exotic for a change, and it's one of the things I miss most about London. I can't just pop out for a kebab when I feel like it, although there is a half-decent Indian restaurant in Upper Bulford."

He told Debbie of his ghostly encounter with May, and showing her the sepia photograph said, "I thought we could use it on the cover, what do you think?"

"Good idea, she's very pretty," she agreed, and suggested "perhaps you could add a paragraph at the end to say how she led you to find it." When they had finished their bottle of wine Debbie had a wander round the garden and, marvelling at the big gothic windows, asked "Didn't you tell me this used to be a woodcutter's cottage?"

"Yes, that's right. That was May's father."

"It's a bit OTT for a humble woodcutter wouldn't you say?"

"Yes, it's funny, but I thought that too," agreed Damian, "and I'm going to have a look at the old records for Bulford Manor. Jed tells me they're now kept at the library in Upper Bulford, so I'll let you know what ever I find out."

On Monday Damian took himself off to the public library to search through everything they had on Bulford Manor. He found out that the original house had been built in the time of King Henry VIII as a hunting lodge, but in the eighteenth century it had been greatly enlarged and altered. Then, in 1830, the lord of the manor had built a folly in the grounds, in the gothic style, but there was no clue why, and Damian seemed to have come to a dead end. However, the librarian had some surprising news, and told him that one of the Bulfords was still alive and living in a nursing home.

She was the youngest sister of the late squire, a Miss Dorothy Bulford, and though she was in her late nineties, she still had all her wits about her. Damian wondered if she could shed some light on the matter, and decided to go and visit her.

The Laurels Nursing Home was a few miles north of Upper Bulford, and Damian went without making an appointment in the hope of being allowed to speak to Miss Bulford. The receptionist was a bit dubious at first, asking if he was a relative, but Damian said, "No, I'm just doing some research on Bulford Manor and I wondered if I could have a little chat with Miss Bulford."

"I'll see if she's up to receiving visitors, if you could wait here please," she told him, and after a few moments she returned and said, "Yes, that would be alright, but don't stay too long, she gets very tired these days."

Damian was shown into a large, cheerful sitting room where a few of the residents were gathered, either reading or dozing in their chairs, and he was taken over to Miss Bulford who was seated by the fire and she smiled as he walked over and introduced himself. "How lovely to have a visitor," she exclaimed with delight, "and such a handsome one too! Come and sit next to me, my dear, how can I help you?"

"Well, I recently bought Honeysuckle Cottage, and I'm writing a book about the lady that used to live there, perhaps you knew her, May Turner?"

"Of course I remember poor May. That was such a tragedy."

"I knew that her father was a forester on the estate, but I wondered if you could tell me a bit more about the history of the cottage, it seems rather eccentric for a workman's cottage."

Miss Dorothy laughed and said, "That's because it was never intended for a worker. My great grandfather had it built for his mistress, and there was a big scandal

153

about it at the time. Her name was Amelia Hobson, and she was the wife of one of the big landowners in the area, and an accomplished portrait painter. My great grandfather hired her to paint the portraits of his children, and they fell in love. It was said that she couldn't have children of her own, that she was barren, but when she started the affair with my ancestor, she became pregnant. Of course, she then realised it was her husband who was infertile, but as she hadn't had relations with him for some time, her husband knew she'd been unfaithful and threw her out."

Damian was fascinated, and said, "That's terrible, what on earth happened to her?"

"She went to see my great grandfather of course, but he wouldn't leave his wife, so then he paid for her to stay in lodgings until the cottage was finished. He'd had those big windows put in so she could do her painting, and he kept her close at hand so that he could pop over to see her and the child any time he fancied."

"Quite a good arrangement really," laughed Damian, "but what did his wife have to say?"

"I don't know if she knew," mused Miss Bulford, "but if she did, then she certainly didn't let on. Amelia had another child by him you know."

"Really?" Damian was intrigued. "What became of those children?"

"Well, the first was a girl, and she married a local farmer, what was his name?" Miss Bulford racked her brains, and then triumphantly came up with the name. "Fuller, that was it!"

"Not a relation to Jed Fuller?"

"Why yes - his great grandfather. How is Jed?"

"He's fine; he gardens for me and keeps me up to speed on the goings on in the village."

"He was sweet on May you know?" Miss Bulford confided. "He wanted to marry her once, but she had another young man at the time."

"Yes, I know, it was very sad. What happened to the other child, was it a boy?"

"Yes, it was a boy, but he died young of a fever and then a couple of years later poor Amelia died in childbirth. My great grandfather was heartbroken and the house stood empty for years, but my brothers and I used to play there as children, and then my grandfather decided to renovate it and let the forester use it, and the rest is history."

Damian had been fascinated by what she had to say and thanked her for her invaluable help. He promised to send her a copy of his book when it was published, and then drove back to Lower Bulford, stopping on the spur of the moment at the tea-shop. The owner, Lizzie Appleby, greeted him with surprise. "We don't see you in here very often, how are you settling in at the cottage?"

"Fine thanks, I really love living there." He looked around and noticed a couple of familiar watercolours on the wall and said, "I see you still have some of Rosa's pictures."

"Yes, sadly that's the last two," Lizzie sighed. "I really miss her, and her work was so in demand." One of the watercolours was a view of his cottage from the bottom of the garden, with a clump of foxgloves in the foreground, and Damian decided he could not bear to leave it there. He also bought a card for Miss Bulford, a front view of Honeysuckle Cottage, writing a little note to thank her for her help.

When he next saw Jed he told him he had been to see the Squire's sister, and that his great grandmother was the love child of the Squire Bulford at that time. "Well I'm jiggered!" Jed exclaimed. "I never knew I had noble connections, but that do explain why the late Squire always looked out for me, he must have known we was related." Jed laughed delightedly, "Just wait till I tells the wife, she'll have to curtsey to me now!"

Chapter 20

The months passed very quickly, and by spring Damian had finished his book. Debbie was delighted and told him "It's the best thing you've ever done, and if this doesn't become a bestseller, I'm a Dutchman!" The publishers were also very upbeat about the book's prospects, and to publicise it Debbie had arranged an airing on Radio Four. There was a phone-in afterwards, and the first call was from a woman called Doreen Smith.

"Hello Mr Shaw," she said eagerly, "I just wanted to say how much I enjoyed your book. May Turner was my aunt, and although I never met her, you really made her come to life for me. Where did you find the picture of her that was on the cover?" Damian told her how May's ghostly presence had shown him where the photograph was lodged between the floorboards, and Doreen said, "Yes, I was sometimes aware of her presence when I lived at the cottage, but I always felt she was very sad."

The next two calls were also from women who had enjoyed the book, but then there was a call from a man who just gave his name as Rupert and said brusquely, "Good morning Mr Shaw. I have just one question for you, how did you manage to con a sick old lady into selling her cottage to you so cheaply?"

Damian was mortified, and for a moment was speechless. The presenter, seeing his discomfort, quickly stepped in and said, "I'm sorry, but we're restricting this programme to questions about the book," and swiftly cut him off.

Damian, regaining his composure, asked if he could reply to the caller, and the presenter nodded assent.

"I think that was the son of the lady from whom I bought the cottage. She was dying and wanted a quick sale, and she wanted someone who would care for the cottage and who would allow her to stay on for as long as she was able. She did have the cottage valued, but she only wanted enough money to pay for her care, and she obviously thought her son would sell her home to the highest bidder regardless of her wishes."

The next day the papers were full of the story, and book sales rocketed. Damian was delighted, for Rupert Montford's malicious phone call had achieved the very opposite effect to what he had intended.

At a book-signing a few days later, Damian saw a handsome young man waiting in the queue. He could not take his eyes off him and, as the man's turn came and he gave his name as Sean, Damian could not prevent his hand from trembling slightly as he signed his name. Later, after he had finished signing all his books, Damian saw that the young man was still hanging around, so he went over to speak to him and asked, "Is there anything you'd like to ask me about the book?"

Sean grinned and replied, "Not about the book, no..." and whispered something rather suggestively in Damian's ear. It had been quite a while since Damian had been on a date with a stranger, so he blushed a little at what was suggested, but happily agreed.

After a lusty night at his hotel where neither of them got much sleep, Damian was thoroughly smitten and begged to see the young man again the following night. Sean was a good ten years younger, had the physique of Michelangelo's David, and Damian would have done anything to keep this young god for himself.

They had arranged to meet at a gay bar, but when Damian arrived a little late, Sean was agitatedly pacing up and down outside. "Thank Christ you've got here at last," he greeted him. "We'll have to go somewhere else, as my boyfriend's inside, and he's spitting mad because I was out all night!"

Damian's heart sank and he said, "I didn't know you were in a relationship," but then his spirits lifted again as Sean replied, "I was, but it's not been good for some time. I told him this morning I want to finish it, but he's the jealous type and I'm scared of what he'll do."

Damian thought quickly and said, "Look, why don't we go round and get your stuff now, and you can stay with me at my cottage; he'll never find you there." It didn't take long to pack up Sean's few possessions, and within the hour they were in the car and heading out of town towards Lower Bulford.

"What a dinky little house!" Sean exclaimed as Damian nosed the car down the narrow lane and pulled up outside Honeysuckle Cottage. Damian showed him round and then made a light supper and opened a bottle of wine, which they then proceeded to finish in the comfort of his double bed.

Next morning as Damian, dressed only in his boxer shorts, was preparing breakfast, Sean came running stark naked down the stairs, snaked an arm round Damian's waist and nuzzled his neck affectionately. Damian had never broadcast in the village the fact that he was gay, and there was nothing camp about the way he spoke or behaved, unlike Sean, who openly flaunted his sexuality. However, Damian had forgotten it was Jed Fuller's day for working in the garden, and he now stood there looking at them open-mouthed, transfixed for a moment or two, before almost slicing into his toes as he dropped the spade in shock. Then, turning tail, he hurried up the lane as fast as his old legs would carry him, heading straight for the Bulford Arms, where he panted, "Get me a double whisky, quick!"

"What's up Jed?" asked one of his drinking pals, "you look like you've seen a ghost."

"It's worse'n that! That Mr Damian's a bleedin' shirt-lifter. He's got some young bloke up there, stark bollock naked he was, and they was canoodling all round the kitchen, it fair turned my stomach!"

"Didn't you know he was gay then?"

"No I bloody didn't," Jed said indignantly "and I'm not ruddy well going back there neither."

His pal winked at the barman and said, "I don't reckon you've got much to worry about in that department Jed, if he hasn't made a pass at you by now, it probably means that he doesn't fancy you."

There was raucous laughter in the bar, and Jed bridled a little. "Well, 'taint natural, is it?"

"There's a lot of it about, me old mate, I reckon you'll just have to turn a blind eye."

"Yeah, and keep me back to the wall," muttered Jed sulkily. He did go back, but made his disapproval very plain, and there were no more afternoons of tea and chats round the kitchen table. Damian was rather saddened, for he had looked on Jed Fuller as a friend.

After a few idyllic weeks at the cottage, Sean was beginning to get on Damian's nerves. He had a habit of smoking dope, which he did continually, and whereas Damian was not averse to the occasional spliff at a party, the constant use was making Sean lazy and dull witted. If Damian tried to start a discussion on some book or film they'd seen, Sean would just agree with everything he said, or yawn and say "Boring!" which made Damian mad. He'd owned cats who were more stimulating company.

Apart from smoking the weed, Sean had no real interest in anything but himself, and would spend hours preening in front of the mirror or lie out in the garden to top up his tan. He sunbathed naked, much to Jed's disgust, and if he didn't get his dope he became bad-tempered and sulky. In desperation Damian had once resorted to asking Jed if he knew anyone at the pub who sold marijuana, but Jed had looked at him coldly and said sternly, "I don't hold with drugs."

When his agent Debbie phoned with an idea she wanted to mull over with him, Damian jumped at the chance to get away from the claustrophobic atmosphere of the cottage.

"Can't I come too?" asked Sean sulkily, but Damian was adamant, "No, sorry, but Debbie's only got a tiny spare room, and we've got business to discuss. Surely you can fend for yourself for a couple of days?"

"I suppose so, if I must" agreed Sean moodily, and he made it plain that he was not at all happy at being left to his own devices.

Damian drove off early next morning with a cheerful "Bye, see you tomorrow night", but Sean merely grunted and pulled the covers over his head. He dozed until midday, when hunger pangs forced him to get out of bed and make himself a cup of coffee and raid the fridge for something to eat. There was bacon, half a dozen eggs and a hunk of cheese, and Sean, too idle to cook the bacon for a sandwich, cut himself a large slice of the cheese which he munched with an apple.

He lay out in the garden and, because he had nothing better to do, began to leaf through Damian's book. He couldn't be bothered to read it all, just skimmed over bits here and there, but he when he came to the chapter on the ghost he laughed out loud. Surely Damian didn't really believe in ghosts? They were just figments of the imagination, and he would certainly give him stick about that when he saw him again. Eventually, tired of reading, he fell asleep, but when he awoke the sun had gone and he felt chilled. He decided a nice hot bath would warm him up and, as he wallowed in the steamy water, he mulled over what he would do later that evening.

It was a toss-up between walking down to the pub and having something to eat there, or he could take a cab into Upper Bulford and see if could find some congenial company. There were no gay clubs but some of the pubs had live music and he would almost certainly be able to get some dope. It all depended on how much money he could scrape together, and he would make sure to look in Damian's sock drawer in case he had hidden a couple of notes in there. Jumping out of the bath, he briskly towelled himself dry and put on his dressing gown, for the bathroom seemed suddenly very chilly.

Deciding he needed a shave he went over to the wash basin and picked up his razor. The mirror was all steamed up so, wiping the condensation with the sleeve of his robe, he was startled to see the terrifying face of a woman looking over his shoulder. Half of her face was horribly disfigured, and her one good eye glared balefully at him, while her mouth seemed frozen in an evil snarl. Sean dropped the razor in shock and whipped round, but there was no-one there. He turned back to the mirror and felt the hairs on the back of his neck prickling, but the apparition had vanished, and for a moment he seemed to be rooted to the spot. Then, at last, he was able to move, and ran in terror to the bedroom where he flung on some clothes, and then rushed from the cottage down to the safe normality of the pub.

"A large brandy please," he panted and it was only as the barman poured it that Sean realised he had come out without his wallet and keys. Looking round he saw Jed Fuller, and approached him in relief. "Jed, you couldn't lend me some money till tomorrow, could you? I promise I'll pay you back."

"No, I'm afraid I couldn't," said Jed coldly, for he had no time for Damian's young friend.

"Please Jed. I've locked myself out," he begged. "I've no money and that ghost scared the pants off me."

"What ghost?" asked Jed, suddenly intrigued, for no-one had actually seen a ghost before, although May had often made her presence felt. When Sean described what he had seen, Jed knew immediately it was May, and it was obvious that the young man was frightened out of his wits. "I can't lend you no money, but I'll make sure the landlord knows that Mister Damian will pay your bill tomorrow."

"Thanks Jed," said Sean gratefully, and then asked the landlord if they had a room for the night as he was too afraid to go back to the cottage on his own.

Luckily there was a vacancy, and after he'd eaten Sean phoned Damian and told him what had happened, begging him to return as soon as possible. He arrived at noon the following day and, after settling up with the landlord, took Sean back to the cottage. "Please can we move back to London, Damian? I'm really scared that awful woman will come back, and besides, I'm so bored here, there's nothing to do."

"That's because you haven't bothered to find a job," said Damian in exasperation.

"Well, there's not exactly a great deal of opportunity around here, is there?" whined Sean, and Damian had to agree, and promised him that they would move back to Chelsea when the flat became vacant at the end of the month. "Chelsea!" exclaimed Sean, "that's brilliant. I've always wanted to live near the King's Road."

If it wasn't for Sean's stunning good looks and prowess in the bedroom, Damian would have ended their relationship, but he hoped that once they moved back to London and the stimulating company of friends, he would finally get off his backside and find himself something to do.

Jed had mixed feelings when Damian told him he was going back to London. He would be kept on to do the garden, but instead of twice a week he would only be required to go in twice a month, and he would miss the money. He most definitely would not miss Sean though, for sensing the old man's disapproval, he camped it up outrageously, baiting him every time he saw him, until Damian told him sternly to behave himself.

A few days back in London, and Damian was back to his bad old ways, going out partying nearly every night, and getting very little work done. Luckily Debbie, his agent, had come up with a brilliant idea. Based on his book, she suggested bringing out a range of Honeysuckle

Cottage house-wares, things like place mats, storage jars and tea towels and other related items. They would all bear the image of the cottage as painted by Rosa, coupled with the photograph of May that had graced his cover. Damian was all for the idea and, with some clever advertising, the things were flying off the shelves, and he was raking in handsome royalties.

Life couldn't have been better, until Damian had a bit of an accident. He had put on a fair bit of weight while he had been living his sedentary lifestyle at the cottage, and so had felt the need to renew his membership at the gym. He had been working out rather too enthusiastically when he slipped and badly wrenched his back. Next day he hobbled round to the doctor's surgery, where he was prescribed strong painkillers, but after a few days when his back was no better, he was worried that he would become hooked on the pills. He decided to seek an alternative treatment, and in the newsagent's window saw a card that offered aromatherapy massage and crystal healing by a woman calling herself Daisy. As luck would have it, she was based around the corner in World's End, so Damian phoned straight away for an appointment and was lucky enough to get a cancellation for the following day.

The treatment room was on the first floor over a book shop, and as soon as Damian entered he was aware of a feeling of calm and tranquillity. Daisy was an attractive woman in her mid thirties, with chestnut hair tied back in a bright scarf, and dressed in a loose, pyjama-style suit. She greeted him with a smile and asked him to strip to the waist and lie face down on the treatment table, where his face fitted into a padded hole through which he could see a large amethyst crystal.

The room was softly lit with scented candles burning on a low table, and peaceful, meditative music was playing as Daisy asked him to breathe deeply and relax. She poured a little warm, aromatic oil onto his back and proceeded to massage it in with deep, firm strokes. At first it was rather uncomfortable, but as his muscles relaxed he began to enjoy it. After a time, Daisy placed heated stones in strategic places on his back, and surrounded him with crystals.

He slept for a few minutes, lulled by the music and the warmth from the stones, and then it was time for the next client, and he reluctantly had to take his leave. His back felt a lot better, and he made another appointment for the following week. After another couple of treatments his bad back was cured, but he enjoyed the massages so much that he decided to continue with them on a regular basis.

A few weeks later he arrived for his appointment to find Daisy rather distracted and not her usual tranquil self. The massage was a little disappointing too, not as good as he had been used to, but he told himself "Everyone has an off day," and asked to make another appointment for the following week.

"I'm not sure I'll be here next week," said Daisy sadly and he, fearing she was ill, asked if there was something wrong. To his dismay she burst into tears and told him that her lease expired at the end of the week, and the greedy landlord had more than doubled the rent. She had a tiny one-bedroom flat above the shop and she sobbed, "I just can't afford it, I only just make ends meet as it is," she told him in despair, "and I don't know what I'm going to do. Everywhere round here is so expensive."

Damian thought for a moment, then said, "I have a cottage you could rent, if you don't mind being out in the sticks. It's a very pretty place and quite peaceful, and I wouldn't charge you very much rent."

"I don't suppose it matters where I go," Daisy replied. "I just can't afford to stay around here."

"Tell you what, why don't I run you down at the weekend?" Damian offered. "And then you can see what you think of it."

DAISY

Chapter 21

Doreen hurried in from the garden to answer the phone, for she had been expecting a call from the nursing home where her mother, Violet, was gravely ill, but the voice at the other end of the line soon brought a smile to her face. "Hello Mummy."

"Daisy, darling, how lovely to hear from you," she cried "I was only thinking about you last night. How is everything?"

"Not so good Mum. I'm afraid I have to move out of my premises."

"Oh, that's a shame, but I thought you were doing so well."

"Well, I was," said Daisy ruefully, "but the bloody landlord's put the rent up sky high, and I can't afford to stay there and I can't find anywhere else that's reasonable."

"I'm sorry to hear that," Doreen sighed, "maybe your father and I could help out a little…"

"Oh no, that's not why I've called," Daisy said quickly. "I just wanted to let you know that I'm moving out of London. One of my clients has a cottage in the country that he'll rent to me quite cheaply, and he's taking me to see it tomorrow."

"That's a stroke of luck darling, so where is this cottage then?"

"It's in a place that I've never even heard of, a village called Lower Bulford."

"What! I don't believe it," cried Doreen in amazement. "I used to live there before you were born. What's the address?"

"Just Honeysuckle Cottage, I think."

"But that's incredible!" Doreen cried. "Talk about a coincidence! That was our home for a while, and we lived there when you were a tiny baby. Before that it used to belong to your Great Aunt May, and when she died she left it to me in her will."

"How amazing!" replied Daisy. "Damian told me that the cottage was very pretty, but why on earth did you sell it?"

"Oh it was in an awful state. It had never been modernised and was damp, with no electricity or hot water, and I had to wash all your nappies by hand," her mother told her, "and I'm afraid I just couldn't cope with that, and your father and I never had the money to bring it up to date."

"Well, now I know that it was your cottage, I really can't wait to see it!"

On the drive to Lower Bulford Daisy told Damian that Honeysuckle Cottage had once belonged to her mother, and he said, "What a remarkable coincidence, Rosa must have bought it from her. I know she spent a fortune doing it up, but it was a real wreck when she got it. By the way, did I tell you before, that the cottage has a ghost? I hope it won't put you off."

"Really, do you know who it is?" asked Daisy, intrigued at the thought of a haunted house.

"Yes, I actually wrote a book about her life, and her name was May Turner."

Now it was Daisy's turn to be astonished, as she learned that the cottage was haunted by the spirit of her Great Aunt May.

Daisy, like Damian and Rosa before her, instantly fell in love with Honeysuckle Cottage as soon as she saw it. Jed had kept the garden neat and tidy, but as Damian had not told him they were coming, had not lit the range, and the interior was rather chilly. It did not matter to Daisy, who was enchanted by everything she saw, the only worry being how isolated the cottage was. "Do you think people will find me here?" she asked Damian anxiously.

Damian shrugged and said, "I don't know, but if you like you could rent it for a trial six months to see how you get on."

He suggested they go for tea in the village, and introduced her to Lizzie Appleby. "I'm so glad the cottage is going to be lived in again, and I'm definitely going to book an appointment with you," said Lizzie enthusiastically, and Daisy warmed to her immediately and told her that it had been her great aunt who used to live in the cottage.

"How extraordinary!" cried Lizzie. "Well, you'll have to meet Jed. He was a good friend to May and he'll be able to tell you all about her."

When they had finished their tea Daisy asked Lizzie if she could leave some cards in the tea rooms to advertise her services. Lizzie nodded and said, "Of course, and you should also ask at the Manor Hotel. They have all sorts of conferences and themed holidays there, and I would have thought your aromatherapy massages would go down a treat."

As they walked back to the car Damian asked, "So you'll definitely rent the cottage then?"

"Yes please. It just feels so right, and I have a hunch it will work out fine for me."

Daisy moved in the following week and Damian had phoned Jed in advance to let him know so that he would light the range and lay in a good supply of logs. After a couple of days, when she had settled in, Jed called round to introduce himself and ask if she needed anything, but when she opened the door he was struck dumb for a moment. "Sorry, I thought you was a ghost for a minute," he stuttered "you'm look so much like May Turner what used to live here."

Daisy laughed, "She was my great aunt, and you I take it are Jed?"

"That's me! It's right nice to see the cottage lived in again, especially by a nice young lady like yourself."

Daisy made a pot of tea and set out some carrot cake, and Jed was putty in her hands. She told him she did massage, and Jed looked at her sideways, guffawed and said, "Do you now?"

"Not that kind of massage, Jed," Daisy laughed, putting him straight. "It's aromatherapy and crystal healing. Perhaps you'd put the word out around the village, and if anyone's got a bad back or stiff neck, send them round to me."

Jed cleared his throat and said tentatively "Well, as it happens, I've got a bad back, chronic it is. How much do you charge?"

"Usually £10 for half an hour," replied Daisy, and when he looked shocked she added quickly "but I'll give you a session for free."

Jed's eyes lit up and he asked eagerly "Really, when could you do it?"

"Now if you like."

She led the way upstairs and showed Jed into the front bedroom where she had set up her massage table. Lighting a few candles, she asked him to strip to the waist, and she would be back in a moment. She quickly changed into her work clothes, and when she returned he was lying on his back on the table.

"You'll have to turn round Jed," she smiled, "and put your face into the hole."

"I won't be able to breathe like that," he protested, but she brushed aside his fears and he meekly did as he was told. As she began to massage Jed with the scented oils he grumbled, "Huh, this smells like a tart's boudoir."

"I wouldn't know," replied Daisy crisply, and after a while he began to relax and enjoy the treatment. When she applied the heated stones he was snoring, and she covered him over and let him sleep for a few minutes before waking him, but when he sat up, he looked startled, grew pale and pointed towards the door. "She's there! Look, 'tis May!"

Daisy turned quickly and thought she saw the shadowy outline of a woman, and suddenly the candles flickered wildly, but then the next moment the apparition had vanished and the candles burnt normally again.

"It was definitely her," said Jed softly, "I ain't never seen her before, but I felt sometimes that she was around nearby." He smiled at Daisy and said, "She were my friend, and I reckon she would have been right proud of you." He got down and stretched himself carefully, saying, "Ooh, that feels much better, I'll definitely recommend you down the pub."

After he had gone Daisy sat and meditated for a while, and again sensed May's presence, but also a prevailing sense of sadness. Soon the feeling began to overwhelm her, so she decided to contact her friend, Anna, who was a spiritual medium and would be able to free a trapped soul.

Next morning, she picked up the phone and dialled her number, and when her friend answered she said, "Hi Anna, it's Daisy. How do you fancy a weekend in the country?"

"Love to darling, but I'm not free till the end of the month."

"That's alright, but I really need your help. The cottage I'm renting has a ghost who I think is my great aunt, and she seems to be giving out so much sadness. I'd really like you to send her over." Anna was skilled at freeing earthbound souls and sending them to the place they were supposed to be, and she agreed immediately.

"You're not scared are you Daisy?"

"Oh no, not at all," Daisy reassured her, "it's just that I'm picking up on her vibes, and it's making me feel sad too."

They made arrangements for Anna to come and stay for a couple of days after two weeks, and then she felt a whole lot better knowing that her aunt would soon be free of her earthly ties.

To take her mind off the ghostly presence, Daisy decided to concentrate on advertising her services, and walked up to Bulford Manor Hotel and asked to speak to the manager, who turned out to be young, female, and very efficient. "Jane Stewart, what can I do for you?" Daisy told her what she did and asked if she could leave some of her cards in reception. The manageress said, "I think we could really do with someone like you on the premises. We already offer a variety of beauty treatments, and we have a sauna and solarium, and I think aromatherapy would be a very welcome addition. Would you be able to work weekends?"

"Oh yes, I could do any days you want," Daisy said eagerly, for she hadn't expected such a positive response. However, she needed to go into the details of everything, and they made an appointment for the following day to discuss finances and the best days for her to work.

Chapter 22

Daisy had arranged to meet Jane Stewart at a quarter past twelve in reception, and was promptly taken down to the basement where she was shown a small, empty room next to the solarium. It had once been used for storage, but it was large enough to accommodate her massage table and it was quiet, which was her main concern, so she asked how much rent she would be charged. "Well, I was thinking of taking a percentage of your earnings rather than you paying us rent, at least for the first few months, see how you get on. What do you normally charge?"

"£10 for half an hour," replied Daisy, and Jane raised an eyebrow and said quickly "Oh, I think we can do better than that. Clients would be prepared to pay at least £18, and if we say you take two-thirds and we take one, would that be acceptable to you?"

"Oh yes, that would be fine," Daisy said eagerly, and Jane asked if she was free for lunch where they could continue their discussion in the hotel restaurant.

Over a pleasant meal Jane told her, "We get a lot of weekend bookings, couples coming for romantic breaks, hen and stag nights, and then we do special breaks such as painting and creative writing courses, and historic tours, that kind of thing, so I think working Fridays, Saturdays and Sundays are essential, and then you can please yourself about which other days you want to work."

"That would suit me fine," Daisy told her "but I have already arranged for a friend to stay for the weekend in two weeks time, and it's not something I can change, so would that be alright?"

Jane laughed, "It'll have to be, but would you be able to start this Friday then?"

"Yes, but there is a slight snag, I need to get my massage table over here somehow and I've no transport."

"No problem, I'll get Sam Fuller to pick it up from you tomorrow morning."

About ten o'clock the following morning, a battered white van pulled up outside the cottage and a lean dark haired man of about fifty got out and rapped at the door. When Daisy opened up he said, "Sam Fuller, come to pick up a table."

"Oh yes, come in," Daisy said and asked curiously "are you by any chance related to Jed?"

Sam grinned and said, "Oh, you've met him then? He's my old man; now where's this table I'm meant to fetch?"

"Upstairs, on the right; the legs fold up so you should be able to manage it." She was struck by the resemblance to Jed, the same lean frame and the brown, weathered skin of someone who worked outdoors, but Sam also had something of the gypsy about him. Perhaps it was the gold ring in his ear, or the rakish way he smiled, but Daisy felt rather drawn to him.

As she showed him into the massage room he nodded approvingly. "Nice room Miss, it feels kind of peaceful."

"That's the whole idea, and you can call me Daisy."

He smiled, showing white, slightly crooked teeth, and said, "Pretty name, it suits you."

She grinned back at him saying, "I've always thought it was a cow's name, I hope that's not what you meant?"

He laughed and said, "No, 'course not. I just meant daisies are kind of pure and simple, and they bring a smile to your face, at least they do to mine."

He was looking at her appreciatively and she suddenly felt embarrassed and said, "That's all right then. Can you manage the table?"

"Yep, no problem, you'll have to give me a massage sometime. Dad said you did wonders for his bad back."

When he had gone she felt strangely elated. There had definitely been a sort of chemistry between them, and she hoped she would be seeing a lot more of him.

Daisy was to see him sooner than she thought for later, taking some things over to the Manor, she asked Jane where she could buy some paint. "You'll have to go to Upper Bulford for that. Do you have a car?"

"No, I've no means of transport at the moment."

"Well, there is a bus twice a day," Jane mused "though I'm afraid you've missed it. However, Sam's going to cash-and-carry for me later, and I'm sure he won't mind giving you a lift."

On the trip into town Sam asked her why she had moved to the village, and she told him about the landlord putting up the rents and how London was too expensive for her to stay.

"I was so lucky to have Damian Shaw as one of my clients," she confided, "and he kindly offered to rent me Honeysuckle Cottage very cheaply."

"What about your boyfriend, couldn't he have helped you out with the rent?"

"I don't have one at the moment. There was someone for a while, but we broke up a couple of years ago."

He looked at her in disbelief and said, "I don't understand what's wrong with those London fellows, fancy leaving a pretty girl like you on her lonesome."

Daisy didn't want to talk about her love life, or rather lack of it, so to change the subject she said quickly "What does your wife do?"

Sam's face suddenly closed up, and he said curtly "My wife's dead."

"Oh, I'm sorry, I had no idea. What happened to her?"

"Cancer," he retorted.

She apologised again and then fell silent, embarrassed, not knowing what to say, but suddenly he put a hand on her arm and said, "It's okay, you weren't to know. I've got three kids though, two boys and a girl, and I'm going to be a granddad soon."

"That's nice," said Daisy, but he laughed ruefully, "Yeah, except it makes me feel my age, and poor old Jed's going to be a great granddad!"

He dropped her off at the town centre saying he would meet her in the Red Lion in forty minutes. She enjoyed looking round the shops and chose some paint in a soft lilac colour that would be restful, then purchased a new CD player for her treatment room and stocked up on scented candles. He was already waiting for her in the bar and, as they sat down with their drinks, asked her if she liked Indian food.

"I love curry. I practically lived on it at one time."

"Good, 'cause there's a half-decent Indian restaurant up the road, and I wondered if you fancied going out for a meal one night?"

Daisy said she'd love to, and then Sam looked at his watch and said they had better head back, so quickly finishing their drinks, they drove back to the Manor where Jane was waiting impatiently for the boxes of wine from the cash-and-carry.

Daisy began to paint the treatment room, and as she had chosen a water-based paint that dried quickly, the job was soon completed and she was able to get back to the cottage before dark. She was a little nervous about walking down country lanes at nightfall, especially when the vixens started calling, for their screams sounded to her like someone being horribly murdered. After living in the city she could not get used to the pitch blackness of the countryside, for there were no streetlights along the way to her cottage, and she shivered suddenly and decided that she would have to get herself some form of transport.

As she prepared her evening meal, she thought about Sam. He was attractive, but a bit older than she would have liked, but then she knew that there wasn't a great deal of choice in this small community, and she couldn't afford to be too picky. He intrigued her however, and she really was quite keen to get to know him better. When she had eaten she suddenly felt very weary and decided to go to bed and read for a while, but she had

179

barely managed a chapter before her eyes began to close and, turning out the light, she slept soundly.

About two o'clock in the morning she woke suddenly to find that her bedroom felt incredibly cold, and thinking that she had left a window open, she pulled back the curtain, but the window was closed. The light of the full moon that now flooded the room revealed a shadowy figure standing at the end of her bed.

"Who's there? May, is it you?" she asked nervously. "What do you want?"

The figure was silent, but Daisy was suddenly overwhelmed by such a strong feeling of despair that she gasped, and with trembling fingers, turned on the bedside lamp. Immediately the figure vanished and the feeling lifted, but it had unnerved her and she decided to leave the light burning for the rest of the night.

Chapter 23

Daisy was open and ready for business on Friday and was gratified to have three clients in the afternoon. Saturday and Sunday were even more hectic, but Monday was very quiet, so she offered Jane a complimentary treatment to thank her for arranging everything so quickly. She would have also offered one to Sam, but he was busy, and she didn't see him until the following evening as she was walking home. "Can I give you a lift home?" he asked, as his van drew alongside, and she accepted gratefully. Then, dropping her off, he asked if she would like to go out for a curry on Thursday evening, saying "I'll pick you up at seven."

It had been a long time since Daisy had been out with anyone, but though she was a little nervous, she was really looking forward to seeing Sam again. On Thursday she set off for home early to have a bath and get ready for her date, and by seven she was ravenous, having only had a salad for lunch in anticipation of the rich Indian meal. There was still no sign of him by seven thirty, and she wondered if she had mistaken the time, but when he had not shown up by eight o'clock, she phoned the hotel. "Is Sam still there? Only he was supposed to show up an hour ago"

"No, sorry," the receptionist told her "he left about five-thirty, but I can give you his mobile number."

Daisy tried his mobile phone, but it was switched off, and by now it was obvious that she had been stood up. Furious with him, for she had been looking forward to the meal as much as his company, she vowed not to waste a second thought on him. Changing into her pyjamas and dressing-gown, she opened a can of soup and made some cheese on toast to assuage her hunger, but it was a poor substitute for the delicious meal she had been promised.

Sam had been really looking forward to his date with Daisy and he had never imagined that he would meet anyone like her in the village. She was beautiful and intelligent, and she had an air of vulnerability about her that he found irresistible. What she saw in him he did not know, but there was an undeniable chemistry between them, and she was the first woman that he'd shown an interest in since the death of his wife.

As he let himself into the house, however, his daughter called out anxiously from upstairs, "Dad? Can you come please ooh…" Her voice tailed off in a groan and he raced up to find her sprawled on the bed clutching her stomach.

"Is the baby coming Kirsty?" he asked in trepidation, and she nodded assent.

"How long between contractions?"

"I don't know," she wailed, "do something Dad, I'm in pain here!"

Somehow he managed to get her downstairs and into the van, and then he drove as fast as he dared to get her to the hospital in Upper Bulford. She looked very young and scared, and he reminded her to do the breathing exercises she had learned in antenatal classes to try and ease the panic they were both feeling, and it was with a profound sense of relief on arriving at Casualty that he was able to deliver her into the hands of the professionals. He went to park the van and then called his son-in-law, Kevin, to let him know that Kirsty had gone into labour and to get to the hospital as quickly as possible.

Looking at his watch he saw that it was already five to seven and he was supposed to pick up Daisy at seven. He had her phone number somewhere, and he rifled through his pockets in a panic, but the elusive piece of paper was not there. Suddenly he remembered, it was in his other shirt, the one he put in the wash. *Damn!* he thought, but there was no way that he could let her know what had happened.

Sam entered the hospital to find that Kirsty had already been taken up to the labour ward, and shortly afterwards Kevin and his parents arrived and he went in to her while the rest of them waited anxiously in the corridor.

After a couple of hours Sam said, "What's taking so long?"

Kevin's mother laughed and said, "Oh it can take all night, especially with the first one. You ought to go home and get some rest."

"I'm not going anywhere," replied Sam tartly, miffed that she had somehow suggested he wasn't up to it. He was in need of a cigarette, however, so when Kevin's dad went outside for a smoke, he cadged one and joined him on the pavement. He lit up, drawing the smoke down, but it tasted foul, and after a moment or two he stubbed it out. He had given up smoking after his wife had died of lung cancer, but occasionally, when he was under stress, he gave in to the urge.

After another hour there was suddenly a lot of activity, with plenty of comings and goings, and then Kevin emerged looking ashen and blurted out "There's something wrong with the baby! They think the cord's tangled round its neck and they've got to do a caesarean straight away."

Sam wanted to go in to see his daughter, but he was prevented by a nurse, and punched the wall in frustration. There was nothing to do but wait, and after what seemed like an interminable period, another nurse came out to tell them that Kirsty was fine and they could go in to see her.

"What about the baby?" Sam asked quietly.

"It's hopeful. We've put him in an incubator and the next couple of hours are critical," the nurse said gently.

Kirsty was tearful and very tired, but she would be fine, and after a few moments he excused himself and asked the nurse if he could go to see the baby. "Yes of course," she replied and led him down the corridor to a side ward where his grandson was hooked up to various tubes in the incubator. He looked so tiny, his lips still tinged with blue, and Sam's eyes filled with tears.

"He's a little fighter," the nurse said encouragingly, "and it doesn't hurt to say a little prayer."

Sam hadn't prayed for years, not since his wife had been diagnosed with cancer, and those prayers hadn't been answered, but now he prayed fervently for the life of his little grandson. He went back in to see Kirsty, but she was now fast asleep, so he sat slumped in the corridor and waited until eventually the nurse came and told him to go home. The baby was a lot more comfortable and there was nothing more he could do.

It was three in the morning by the time he fell into bed, and when he awoke it was noon. He drove over to see Jed and Nellie and took them to see Kirsty and the baby, who had improved during the night, and then suddenly he remembered Daisy. She must have been wondering what had happened to him, so when he had dropped his parents back at their home he went straight to the Bulford Manor Hotel to see her. As luck would have it she was busy with a client, and Sam was in two minds whether to wait until she had finished, or go home and call round to see her later in the evening.

He opted to go home and have something to eat as he had missed lunch and his stomach was growling, and once he had eaten his fill and downed two cans of lager, he sat down to watch some television until it was time to go and see Daisy but, still tired out from the previous night, his eyes closed and he slept. When he awoke it was after ten and he wondered if he should go round and offer her his apologies, and deciding not to put it off any longer, he jumped in his van and headed for Honeysuckle Cottage. There were no lights showing in the windows, so either she had gone to bed early, or she was out, so despondently he turned the van round and went back home, and he would try again in the morning.

Daisy had been surprised when there was still no word from Sam the following day, and he had not shown up for work either. She was busy all day, and had firmly put him out of her mind, but Saturday there was a knock at her door at breakfast time, and there he was, standing on the door-step looking very apologetic.

He was about to explain, but before he could get a word out Daisy cut in, saying "Whatever excuse you've got, I'm not interested!" and angrily slammed the door in his face. She watched him get into his van and drive away, and wondered if she had been too hasty, but then thought, "No-one treats me like that again." She had suffered too many humiliating episodes at the hands of her last boyfriend, forgiving him time after time, only to be cheated and lied to over and over, and so had sworn to herself that she would never let a man treat her in that way again.

With a steady flow of clients on Saturday and Sunday, Daisy decided to take Monday off to go shopping. She needed to stock up on food and to order a single bed for when Anna arrived at the weekend, so she caught the early bus into Upper Bulford and browsed around the shops, buying a few more scented candles and a couple of paperback books along the way, until it was time to return home. As she waited for the homebound bus she saw Sam pass by in his van, but either he hadn't seen her, or he had taken her harsh words to heart.

On Tuesday she had a couple of aromatherapy sessions in the afternoon, but she left Wednesday free in order to await the arrival of the bed. It happened to be Jed's day for working in the garden, and as she watched him trim the hedge she thought he was looking a bit tired. He must be in his late seventies, she mused, but though he was a little arthritic, he showed no signs of wanting to retire. She knocked on the window and beckoned him in, saying "You look like you could do with a cup of tea."

He sat down gratefully, glad of the rest, and Daisy set out a plate of biscuits and told him that her friend Anna was going to do an exorcism, and said, "I just feel May is so sad being trapped here and Anna can set her free."

Jed looked a little bemused and asked curiously "Is she a proper psychic then, like can she talk to the spirits?"

"Yes of course," Daisy explained. "She'll ask May what the reason is that's preventing her from moving on, then say an incantation and hopefully send her on her way."

"I don't s'pose I could come along, could I? I won't get in the way or nothing..." Jed asked hopefully, and Daisy said he would be very welcome to join them.

As Jed sipped his tea he asked curiously "What have you and Sam fallen out about? Only he's been in a right foul mood all week."

"Well, he asked me out for a meal and then stood me up," Daisy said crossly, "and he didn't even have the manners to let me know, and in my book that makes him a pig, and you can tell him exactly what I think of him!"

"What night were you s'posed to go out then?"

"Thursday."

"Aah, that explains it!" said Jed in relief, for he didn't think Sam would treat any woman so thoughtlessly. "His daughter Kirsty was rushed into hospital late on Thursday afternoon. She'd gone into premature labour, and then there was some complications with the baby. We thought we'd lost the poor little chap at one stage, but he's alright now, thank goodness."

"I'm sorry to hear that, but he could have phoned me," said Daisy peevishly.

"Oh he meant to, but in all the kerfuffle he lost your phone number, and he was at the hospital all night. Didn't he come round to explain?" Jed said quickly.

Daisy grinned ruefully and said, "He did eventually, but I'm afraid I gave him a bit of a mouthful." She felt a little ashamed that she had not allowed him to explain, and decided that she would try to build bridges with him the next time she saw him, and hoped fervently that he was not too annoyed with her.

Chapter 24

Anna arrived in time for lunch on Saturday, and Daisy was so happy and relieved to see her friend, for May's sad presence was really beginning to affect her and bringing her down. Anna was striking in her looks, tall with a mass of wild, dark hair and a penchant for wearing long flowing clothes. She did look rather fey, but was actually very matter-of-fact about what she did, but the moment she entered the cottage she stopped in her tracks and said, "Oh yes, I can really feel her presence, and you weren't kidding when you said she had an aura of sadness, it's making me feel positively suicidal." She felt so uncomfortable in the house that they decided to go out and have lunch at the pub, where Jed was propping up the bar. Daisy introduced Anna and told him that if he still wanted to attend the séance, to be at the cottage by five.

He arrived promptly, and found that Daisy had lit all the candles in the house and set them around the kitchen.

"I ain't never been to nothing like this," said Jed nervously, "what do I have to do?"

"Nothing, just keep quiet so Anna can concentrate," Daisy told him, "and then we touch hands to form a circle and you mustn't break the circle till it's finished."

They sat around the kitchen table and linked hands and Anna closed her eyes and breathed deeply for a few moments. After a little while she asked "May, if you are with us, please make your presence known." Immediately an icy draught curled round them and the candles on the table guttered wildly. They could feel the tension in the room and Jed licked his lips nervously.

Anna asked "May, do you want to tell us why you haven't moved on?" She was silent for a minute as she waited for the reply then said, "You're scared? What are you afraid of?" The candles flickered again and then she said, "You don't mean scared but scarred?"

"She was terrible scarred from the fire," interjected Jed.

Anna went on "Why would that prevent you from leaving earth?" Again she sat silently, then turned to Jed and asked "Who was James?"

"He was her fiancé, but he ended up marrying her sister, and then he was killed in the war."

"She says she's afraid James will reject her. Hang on, there's another spirit trying to get through..." Anna sat immobile, eyes closed; then said, "It's James, he's telling her not to worry, she will be perfectly whole again and he's waiting for her on the other side and he has her little boy with him, do you hear that May?

Suddenly Jed leapt up and shouted "That's a bloody lie! May never had no child, and I don't reckon you'm a real medium at all."

"Ssh Jed, sit down," Daisy admonished him.

After a moment Anna said, "May says to let Jed know that she was carrying his child and died of a miscarriage, but she was afraid to tell him she was pregnant, and so he mustn't blame himself."

He was stunned by what Anna had told him, and went rather pale, but then suddenly he remembered one wet and windy April day when he had burst into the

190

kitchen at Honeysuckle Cottage to find May taking a bath in front of the fire. "Oh sorry May," he had apologised, "I'll wait out in the shed till you'm finished."

"Don't be silly Jed," May called, "come on in, and you can make yourself useful and scrub my back for me, if you wouldn't mind."

"'Course I don't mind, but why you having a bath at this time of day?"

"I went for a walk and slipped over in the muddy lane."

"You'm didn't hurt yourself, did you?" Jed asked in concern.

She laughed and shook her head. "No, I just got covered in this stinking mud."

He began to soap her back, reflecting how soft and white her skin was there, and before he could stop himself his hands had moved to her breasts and she moaned, "Oh yes, Jed, please make love to me. Just one more time please."

He knew he shouldn't, but he just couldn't help himself, and in a moment of weakness he took her over the kitchen table, and then afterwards was thoroughly ashamed of himself.

Within a few weeks May guessed that she was pregnant, but she couldn't tell Jed. At first she was shocked, but then the realisation of having a child of her own to love was the most wonderful thing to have happened to her. He, or she, would grow up accustomed to her scars and wouldn't be bothered by them, and she would have a companion and someone to care for her in her old age. When she started showing she took to wearing loose, baggy sweaters and Jed, being a man, had never noticed the change in her.

That winter, however, she had caught a terrible chill that went straight to her weakened lungs, and on a freezing cold day Jed had arrived to find her at the kitchen table, a towel over her head, inhaling the mentholated steam to try and ease her breathing. He had wanted to get the doctor to come and visit her, but she was adamant that she didn't want him to come. She was terribly afraid that if he found out she was pregnant, then the baby would be taken away from her, and she would be judged unfit to look after a child.

She had sat beside the fire in her flannel nightgown, wrapped up in her winter coat, and Jed had stoked up the fire and brought in a good supply of logs, before fetching the quilt from her bed. "Now are you'm sure you're warm enough?" he had asked anxiously. "I could help you get up the stairs to bed if you like."

"No, I think it's better for me sitting up," she had wheezed. "I can breathe easier and it's a lot warmer down by the stove."

He had made her a hot, malted drink and then added a good slug of whisky from his hip-flask before taking his leave, saying "I'll pop over first thing in the morning to see how you are."

When he had left she dozed fitfully, but later that night was woken by agonising pains in her stomach. May knew it was too early for the baby to come, as she was only at seven months, and realised that something was very wrong. The fire was low and she attempted to put on some more logs, but as she got up she realised that she was bleeding heavily. At first she had tried to stop the blood with a towel, but there was far too much, and she began to feel weak and dizzy and struggled for breath. She sank down to the floor and managed to pull the quilt over to cover herself, but the pains were getting worse, and then eventually she passed out and the life blood slowly ebbed out of her.

Cycling over the following morning, Jed had a feeling of foreboding, and as soon as he entered the kitchen and saw her lying in front of the cold grate with a bloody towel in her hand, he feared the worst. He touched her face, and she was cold and lifeless and he thought it was her lungs that had haemorrhaged, as he'd no inkling that she was expecting his baby, and he blamed himself for not bringing the doctor to her earlier.

May's funeral was a very quiet affair, with just Jed and Nellie in attendance along with a couple of village women who had once worked with May up at the manor. The day had been wet with a north wind threatening snow, and everyone had been glad to get back to their firesides. Then, a couple of days later, Jed unaccountably found himself cycling over to the cottage. He didn't know what had drawn him, but when he got there he saw May's cat shivering on the doorstep, the other one having disappeared some months previously.

When it saw him it ran to him meowing pitifully, and then he had picked it up and tucked it into his coat. "Poor thing!" Nellie cried when he brought it home. "It must be half-starved." She put down some warm milk and some left-over stew and watched as the hungry cat devoured it, and as soon as she sat down in her chair the little creature had jumped on to her lap and, purring contentedly, curled up to sleep in its new home.

Anna continued with the séance and said, "May, there is nothing to fear. I'm now going to say a prayer to send you over, go to the light where James is waiting for you." She recited a Latin incantation three times, and then suddenly the oppressive feeling of sadness lifted and she smiled and said, "May's gone, she's at peace now."

Jed was silent for a moment, and then said softly "I never knew about the baby. She never said nothing, and we only done it a couple of times, and she was that lonely that I couldn't say no to her." He asked anxiously "You won't tell Sam or Nellie will you?"

"Your secret's safe with me Jed," Daisy said firmly, and then he relaxed and apologised to Anna for doubting her abilities. The mood lifted, with Daisy relieved that her great aunt was finally at peace and Jed happy that his old friend was with her loved ones once more. To celebrate Daisy opened a bottle of sparkling wine and Jed regaled them with stories of when he and May were young, and one story in particular made them hold their sides with laughter.

Jed had been about ten years old, and in the school holidays had gone pond dipping with May and another friend. They had taken jam jars and Jed had a net made out of an old stocking fixed to a wire frame and joined on to a long bamboo pole. He had spotted a beautiful dragonfly, and in his eagerness to catch it, had overbalanced and fallen headlong into the pond.

He had emerged looking like Caliban, covered in green slime and duckweed, and May had laughed till it hurt, but then had urged him to take off his clothes and lay them in the sun to dry. He had baulked at removing his pants though, feeling shy in front of May, so she had sweetly offered to lend him hers to wear until his own were dry.

Jed chuckled "It were the only time I got into her knickers back then, but it sure weren't for the want of trying!"

Eventually it was time for him to go home, and as he left he said to Daisy "Don't be too hard on Sam, he's a good lad, and he deserves a bit of happiness."

Daisy grinned and retorted, "You can tell him if he still wants his complimentary massage, I'm free on Monday!"

Chapter 25

On Monday Daisy was on tenterhooks all day waiting to see if Sam would take up her invitation. She had virtually given up on him, thinking that perhaps her display of bad temper had put him off, but at five o'clock he put his head round the door and said, "Jed tells me you'll give me a complimentary massage. Am I too late, only if you're off home, I can come back another day?"

"No, come in, I wasn't planning on going yet," said Daisy quickly. "I really owe you an apology. Jed told me what happened that Thursday, and I should have given you the chance to explain."

Sam grinned and said, "You were a bit of a hell-cat! I didn't dare stay around in case you hit me with the frying pan."

Daisy laughed, and suddenly the tension lifted between them and she asked, "How's your daughter and the baby?"

"Oh they're fine now, but the little chap cries a lot. Kept me up most of the night."

"Do they live with you then?" asked Daisy curiously.

Sam replied "Yes, for the time being, but only till they get their own place. They were supposed to move into a flat in Upper Bulford, but at the last minute the sale fell through. Kevin, my son-in-law, has gone back to stay with his parents for a while, and Kirsty and the baby are staying with me. It's not easy for youngsters to buy anywhere these days, everything's got so expensive."

"I know what you mean," said Daisy sympathetically, "I had that problem in London. Prices keep going up all the time, but one's earnings never seem to catch up."

She asked Sam to take his shirt off and lie face down on the massage table, and she looked appreciatively at his lean, tanned body as she smoothed the oil into his back. His skin felt warm and smooth beneath her hands and she thought to herself, *I'm going to enjoy this as much as he is.* As she massaged up towards his neck he groaned and she said, "You're very tight up in your shoulders, what have you been up to?"

"I was doing a lot of driving yesterday, and I always get tense on the motorway."

"Well, try and relax and let me ease out those knots."

She worked hard on him, and after half an hour she was done and asked him how he felt. He sat up, flexed his shoulders, then smiled and said, "Fantastic! You've worked wonders." As he put his shirt back on he asked her if she was doing anything that night.

Daisy shook her head, "No, I've got nothing planned, why?"

"I wondered if you fancied going for a curry, seeing as you missed out on it last week?"

"Well, yes, but I need to go home and change."

"No, you don't need to do that; you're fine as you are. Come on," he urged, "the van's outside, and if we go now we'll get served quickly before they get too busy."

On the drive to Upper Bulford Sam explained that though the food was good at the curry house, the service was awful, and when the restaurant was full he'd been known to wait an hour for his meal. Luckily when they arrived it was almost empty, so they were served almost immediately, and Daisy was gratified to find that the food was just as good as she'd been promised. They chatted easily over the meal, Sam telling her about the drama with his daughter's baby arriving early, about his two sons, about Jed, and about his job, and then he said, "That's more than enough about me, and I don't know anything about you, except you give a damn fine massage."

Daisy shrugged and said, "There's not a lot to tell really. I'm single, pushing forty, and I've got a younger brother who I haven't seen for years as he emigrated to Australia, and my parents are still alive and kicking, at least they were last time I looked."

"What made your brother want to go to Australia?"

"Oh Dad and he didn't get on, and I think he just wanted to get as far away as possible."

"Have you ever been married?"

"Almost. I lived with someone for three years when I was at college, and we got engaged," Daisy told him, "but then he was offered a really good job in Saudi Arabia. I didn't fancy going there, and anyway I was taking my finals, but he said the money was too good to turn down, so he went without me. We kept in contact for a while, but then just lost touch, you know how it is."

"Not really, no. I met my wife at school, she got pregnant, and we got wed. There's never been anyone else."

"What, no-one, ever?" teased Daisy.

Sam looked a bit abashed and muttered, "Well, one or two little flings maybe; nothing that mattered. Wasn't there anyone serious after your fiancé?"

"Yes, there was someone," said Daisy, pulling a face, "but the less said about him the better. He was a real bastard and he made me lose all confidence in men, and for a long time I didn't want anything to do with anyone." It had brought back painful memories, and to change the subject Daisy asked Sam if he had ever met her Great Aunt May.

"Yeah, just the once," he replied, "and it was the only time I remember getting a walloping from my dad."

"Why? Whatever did you do?"

"Well, dad was taking me to play football, I guess I was about six or seven, but first he had to drop some groceries off at May's house. He told me to wait outside, but I was a nosy little sod and so I crept in behind him, but when I saw her I just yelled out, I couldn't help myself, and then he told me to get out, and I'd never seen him so angry."

"What made you yell?"

"She looked that terrible, all scarred and with her mouth all crooked, and I thought she was a witch, but later, after he'd thrashed me, dad explained that the reason she looked like that was because she had rescued two boys from a fire and had got badly burned. I felt sorry for her then, but I still had nightmares for weeks afterwards."

After their meal Sam drove her home and she asked him if he'd like to come in for coffee, but he declined, saying "No, not tonight, we're both tired, but I could come round tomorrow night and cook a meal if you like."

Daisy looked at him in surprise and said, "I didn't have you down as the domesticated type."

"Don't judge a book by its cover," he said, grinning at her, "there's a lot about me you don't know yet."

"I look forward to finding out then," she replied, and suddenly he cupped her face in his hands and kissed her, a gentle kiss on the lips, then bade her goodnight. She watched him drive away, and then she was overcome by such a feeling of loneliness that she willed him to turn round and come back to her, but he didn't, and sighing she went upstairs to her empty bed.

The following day Sam picked her up from work, and she asked him what he was going to make for their supper. "Oh, I've already made it, it only needs heating up. It's one of my specials."

"Yeah, but what is it?" asked Daisy curiously, but Sam merely laughed and said, "Wait and see!" He put the pot in the oven along with some garlic bread wrapped in foil, and then opened a bottle of red wine while Daisy set the table.

"I really like this kitchen," said Sam, looking about him appreciatively, "it's very homely."

Daisy asked if he'd like to see over the rest of the cottage, saying "It's not very big, but it suits me perfectly."

She showed him into the sitting room, but it was too dark to see the beautiful garden or get the amazing effect of the light flooding in through the huge windows, so then she led the way upstairs, taking him first into her bedroom. Whether it was the sight of the bed which dominated the room, or the close proximity of Daisy and the aroma of her perfume that gave Sam the urge to kiss her he couldn't say, but he was surprised by the strength of his feelings for her. Suddenly he pulled her into his arms and kissed her, tentatively at first, as he wasn't sure if she felt the same, but she responded eagerly saying, "Hold me Sam." He kissed her again, more passionately this time, pulling her closer, his hands cupping her bottom, and she could feel him hard against her belly. The next moment they were tearing each other's clothes off as they fell onto the bed in a wild, frenzied embrace.

When it was over, they looked at each other in astonishment. "How did that happen?" asked Daisy bemusedly.

"I reckon we were both hungry for it," replied Sam, "and it's been a long time since I've wanted anyone like that."

"Me too," she said.

Sam kissed her gently and laughed, "Well, I don't know about you, but it's given me a real appetite for our dinner. Come on, it'll be ready by now."

He had made a rich stew, with baby onions and carrots, flavoured with marjoram, and Daisy tucked in with gusto, saying "Mm, this is delicious. What is it, chicken?"

"No, rabbit. Shot it myself, and the veggies are home grown too."

"I've never eaten rabbit. I'm glad you didn't tell me before, else I might not have tried it, but it was really good."

"Glad you enjoyed it," Sam said, pouring them another glass of wine. "I reckon we should take these upstairs," he said, giving her a smouldering look, "and then I'll give you your dessert!"

Daisy led the way and lit the candles on the chest of drawers, and then they climbed into her wrought iron bed where Sam began to kiss and caress her gently, exploring her with his lips and tongue, and this time they made love slowly, savouring each other's bodies, until exhausted they slept, entwined in each other's arms.

Chapter 26

Next morning Sam woke to sunlight streaming in through the big arched windows to find Daisy playing with a tendril of hair at the nape of his neck. He turned and smiled at her, kissing the tip of her nose, and said, "Hello my lovely. How're you feeling this morning?"

Daisy stretched and said sleepily, "Wonderful. How about you?"

"After a good night's sleep, I feel like a ruddy teenager again! I don't know what you've done to me girl, but I can't seem to get enough of you." He nuzzled her neck, his hand cupping her breast, and then made love to her again.

They must have dozed off, for soon a loud banging at the door woke them up with a start. Daisy had completely forgotten it was Jed's day for working in the garden and promptly dashed to the bathroom, while Sam ran downstairs dressed only in his underpants. Jed's face was a picture as his son answered the door then a sly smile stole over his features as he said, "So you made up with her then?"

Sam grinned, "You could say that! And I suppose you want a cuppa before you start work?"

Sam began to spend more and more time with Daisy. The cottage was a peaceful haven from the chaos of his own home where his daughter and her husband squabbled constantly, not to mention the baby's incessant crying that was keeping him awake nearly every night. They had developed a routine of Sam cooking for Daisy on Fridays and Saturdays, which were her busiest days, and then once a week they went out to eat, usually to the Indian restaurant in Upper Bulford, although sometimes they had steak at the Bulford Arms. Daisy blossomed with his love and care, and had never been happier, and though Sam was a little older than she would have liked, he was still fit and strong and a caring and considerate lover, and in the end the age difference didn't seem to matter at all.

It is always when life is as good as it can be that fickle fate seems to delight in throwing a spanner in the works, and so it was on a bleak November day that Daisy got a phone call from her mother to tell her that her grandmother had died. They had been expecting it for some time, as Violet Marvel had been terminally ill with cancer, but nonetheless it was still a shock.

Daisy had not been that close to her grandmother since the death of her husband Harry Marvel ten years earlier. She had adored Grandpa Marvel, who had spoiled her shamelessly, and had been devastated when he died suddenly of a heart attack, but Violet had always favoured her younger brother, and in her eyes he could do no wrong.

Never easy to get on with at the best of times, Violet had gone into herself with grief, and had become more querulous and fault finding with everyone around her. Doreen had patiently put up with her mother's moods, but Daisy avoided the company of her grandmother as much as possible, as it seemed that Violet singled her out for the harshest criticism. Doreen said it was because she looked like Violet's sister May, and the resemblance made her grandmother feel guilty about the past.

When Violet developed Alzheimer's, and had become too forgetful and a danger to herself, Doreen had arranged to put her into a care-home. She had felt terribly guilty about this, for her generation had always been taught that one looked after one's own, but her husband Raymond had put his foot down. "If your mother comes here, you won't see me for dust!" He had never really got on with his mother-in-law, so reluctantly Doreen bowed to his wishes, but she still felt guilty, and nothing Daisy could say would comfort her.

After a tearful half an hour trying to console her mother, Daisy was preparing breakfast for herself when the phone rang again, and she was surprised that this time it was her landlord, Damian Shaw. He sounded uncharacteristically nervous as he asked her how she was, and then there was a long pause and much throat clearing.

"What's wrong Damian?" asked Daisy. "I know you haven't just phoned me up to enquire after my health."

He replied in a rush of words, "No, of course not. I'm sorry Daisy, oh gosh, I don't know how you're going to take this, but I'm afraid I've got to sell the cottage."

"No!" Daisy's legs suddenly gave way and she had to sit down before asking "But why?"

"I'm going to Thailand for a few months," Damian told her. "An Australian film company is making a movie based on one of my books, and it's all set in Thailand and Sydney," he explained excitedly "so I really want to be on hand to advise, and I'm afraid I need some money rather quickly, so I've got to give you a month's notice. I'm so sorry Daisy, I know how much you love the cottage, but I wouldn't sell it if I didn't have to."

When she had put the phone down Daisy began to cry. She loved Honeysuckle Cottage and had never been happier, but there was no way that she could afford to buy it, and now her world was falling apart and it was all going to end. She needed to speak to Sam, and as she reached for the phone she prayed that he had not yet left for work. He had spent the night at his own house, offering to baby sit for his daughter and son-in-law, so that they could have a night out, and as he answered the phone he sounded tired. "Daisy, what's wrong?"

"Please Sam, just come, I need to see you," she had begged, and then had burst into tears.

He was there in ten minutes, looking weary and unshaven, and Daisy threw herself into his arms. "Oh Sam," she wailed, "I don't know what to do. Damian's just phoned, he wants to sell the cottage and I've got a month's notice to get out."

"Is that all?" he said, his voice gruff, "I thought it was something serious." He was mock angry with her, as on the drive over he'd thought perhaps she'd had an accident or been attacked.

She went on, "I love this place, and I can't bear to leave here. It's the first place that's really felt like home, and also my gran died today."

"Oh babe, I'm sorry." Sam was immediately solicitous and put his arms round her.

She shook her head, "It's okay, I'm not upset for myself, but Mum's devastated. She was crying on the phone to me this morning, and I can't say anything to comfort her."

Sam made them both a strong cup of coffee and they sat down at the kitchen table. He was silent for a moment, then said, "You could always move in with me, that is, if you'd like to?"

"That would be lovely Sam, but what about your daughter and the baby? There wouldn't be enough room for all of us surely?"

Suddenly he grinned at her and said, "The solution's bloody obvious! Why don't I buy this place for us? The kids can buy my place – then the problem's solved!"

"Sam that would be fantastic!" cried Daisy. "Do you think they would go for it?"

"Yeah, of course they will, they'll bite my hand off. My place isn't much, but it's miles better than that pokey flat they were trying to buy, and at least it's got a bit of a garden for the little 'un to play in."

"Well then, I could pay you the rent and…"

"Don't be so daft," Sam interjected, "I'm buying this for the both of us. Actually…" He hesitated a moment then said, "I was going to ask you something, and I was going to wait till Christmas, but now as things have changed…"

"What was it?" asked Daisy eagerly.

"I was going to ask you if you'd do me the honour of becoming my wife."

Daisy hadn't expected that, and for a moment was lost for words, and Sam continued shyly, "It wasn't meant to be like this babe. I wanted it to be all romantic and proper, and present you with a diamond ring, and here I am all unkempt and bleary-eyed, proposing over a sink full of dirty dishes. Sorry Daisy, I know I'm not much of a catch, but I love you and I'd be right proud if you would be my wife. What do you say?"

Daisy looked up at him, and her eyes were shiny with tears, but this time they were tears of joy, and she cried "I say yes, Sam Fuller!" And then he pulled her into his arms and kissed her, the stubble on his face scratching the tender skin of her cheek, but she didn't care. For the first time she had a man that really loved and cherished her, and at last she would truly be able to call Honeysuckle Cottage her home.

SYNOPSIS of THE SCENT OF HONEYSUCKLE

MAY, VIOLET AND DOREEN

In 1956 Doreen Bland becomes pregnant and is left Honeysuckle Cottage by her Aunt May, a tragic recluse whom she has never met. She gradually uncovers the reasons for her aunt's reticence as she is left horribly scarred after her heroic rescue of the Squire's grandsons, and why her mother and her aunt haven't spoken for years. When she marries her fiancé Raymond, they move into the cottage and she is aware of her aunt's sad, haunting presence, but as the conditions there are too primitive to bring up a baby, they move out and the cottage is left empty for years.

ROSA

The cottage is bought and renovated by Rosa Montford, a middle aged divorcee struggling to become an artist. She too is aware of May's presence, but she seems to have a benign influence, as Rosa's paintings are suddenly in demand. She is befriended by Jed, who helps with the garden and who was May's only friend, and he tells Rosa all about her life. Rosa confides in Jed about her son, Rupert, who has a gambling problem, and when she becomes incurably ill she decides her son is not to have the cottage. She chances to meet Damian Shaw, a writer, and agrees to sell him the cottage cheaply on condition it is not altered, much to her son's chagrin.

DAMIAN

Damian Shaw has a writer's block, and his life as a gay man is a constant social whirl that he feels is preventing him from writing. He falls in love with Honeysuckle Cottage, and when Jed tells him the story of May, he is convinced he has the makings of a best seller. He buys the cottage and begins to write May's story, her ghostly presence showing him where her photograph is hidden between the floorboards. The book is a great success, and on a signing tour meets a young man, Sean, and takes him back to the cottage, much to Jed's disgust.

Sean is terrified by May's ghost and they move back to London. Damian is back to his bad old ways, but when he hurts his back he meets Daisy, an aromatherapist, who gives him healing massages. When her landlord raises the rents she has to move out of town and Damian rents her the cottage.

DAISY

Daisy is Doreen's daughter, and is amazed to learn that Honeysuckle Cottage used to belong to her mother. She finds May's ghostly presence unbearably sad, and arranges for a psychic friend to perform an exorcism. She then has a romance with Jed's son Sam, but things do not run smoothly at first. They get back together, and life is idyllic until Damian calls to say he has to sell the cottage. Daisy is heartbroken, but Sam comes to the rescue by suggesting he buys the cottage and then proposing to Daisy, who happily accepts.